GUNS ALONG

THE MORA

**Center Point
Large Print**

**This Large Print Book carries the
Seal of Approval of N.A.V.H.**

RAY HOGAN

GUNS ALONG

———◆———

THE MORA

CENTER POINT PUBLISHING
THORNDIKE, MAINE

This Center Point Large Print edition
is published in the year 2003 by arrangement with
Golden West Literary Agency.

The text of this Large Print edition is unabridged. In other
aspects, this book may vary from the original edition. Printed in
Thailand. Set in 16-point Times New Roman type by
Bill Coskrey and Gary Socquet.

ISBN 1-58547-314-6

Library of Congress Cataloging-in-Publication Data.

Hogan, Ray, 1908-
    Guns along the Mora / Ray Hogan.--Center Point large print ed.
    p. cm.
    ISBN 1-58547-314-6 (lib. bdg. : alk. paper)
    1. Large type books. I. Title.

PS3558.O3473G815 2003
813'.54--dc21

                                                    2003040955

for . . .
ACKLIN HOOFMAN
Muskegon, Michigan

1

LAVERTY saw the old spotted longhorn burst out of the brush and, head low, wicked needle-sharp horns poised, charge straight for Pettibone, who had just turned away.

"Henry, look out!" he shouted.

Pettibone cut the horse he was riding sharp left. The black stumbled at the abrupt turn and went down, throwing Pettibone from the saddle. Before he could regain his feet the steer was upon him.

Tom Laverty, gun in hand as he rushed in, fired a shot over the longhorn's head. He could take no aim as Pettibone and the steer were a confused, struggling blur. Rushing toward the cloud of swirling dust enveloping his friend and the wild-eyed longhorn, Laverty fired again in the hope of frightening the animal.

"Henry!" he yelled once more.

There was no answer, only the thrashing about at the edge of the brush, the snorting of the steer, and the sound of hooves scuffing the sun-baked ground.

Tom swore and, ignoring the time-honored rule that said a man should never leave his saddle at such times, leaped from his horse and, again firing a shot, hurried toward the haze of spinning dust. Other cowhands, who had been working with him and Pettibone along the San Pedro River that morning rounding up strays for Jeremiah Madden, were now pounding up, yelling questions.

Tom drew back abruptly. The cloud of tan parted suddenly and the old steer plunged out into the open. Red eyes blared wide, lather dripping from his jaws, the ends of his horns stained with blood, he lowered his head again and charged once more—this time at Laverty.

Tom lunged to one side and at close quarters triggered a bullet at the maddened brute. The lead slug struck a horn, ricocheted off the steer's head. The animal staggered slightly and veered off, running unsteadily out onto the flat that edged the river.

Immediately Laverty hurried into the drifting dust. He could see Pettibone lying near the stand of brush, a crumpled, motionless shape. Reaching the man, Tom knelt beside him. Relief filled him. Pettibone was alive.

"What happened?" one of the three cowhands attracted by the gunshots shouted as he rode in close.

"That steer gored Henry," Tom said, and gently turned Pettibone onto his back.

The relief he had felt moments earlier vanished. Blood was oozing from a hole in Pettibone's chest and from another in his side. The old longhorn had given him a vicious mauling.

"Get a wagon—and some blankets!" he shouted to the silently watching riders as he pulled off his neckerchief and drew his bandanna from a hip pocket. "Tell Mrs. Madden to come—and you better tell her what happened so she'll know what to bring."

All three men wheeled away. Laverty folded his neckerchief into a pad and pressed it into the wound in Henry's chest; following a like procedure, he used the bandanna for the second bullet hole.

The hammer of hooves brought Tom around, the thought that one of the riders, for some reason, was returning. He was wrong. It was the old spotted longhorn. The crazed brute had turned about, was charging again.

Tom, crouched, pivoted on a heel and drew his gun. He wasn't exactly certain but he believed he had one, perhaps two bullets left in the weapon. Everything had happened so fast he couldn't remember. Whatever, he had no time to do any reloading.

Steadying himself, he leveled the .45 at the oncoming steer's head, hoping to drive the bullet into the vulnerable spot between the animal's eyes. At the sharp crack of the weapon the steer dropped instantly, his thrashing legs stirring up the dust once again. Laverty sighed in relief; the heavy slug had reached its intended mark.

"Tom—"

Pettibone's weak voice quickly drew Laverty's attention. "Take it easy, Henry," he said quietly. "The boys've gone for a wagon—and Mrs. Madden. Expect we'll have you fixed up real good right soon."

Pettibone's features were slack and all color had drained from his usually ruddy face. "What—what was that shooting?"

"That damned steer came back for another try. Had

to stop him."

"Was a mean cuss. That fool horse of mine had to go and stumble over his own feet, else I—"

"Was something you couldn't help . . . Maybe you best not talk—"

"Kind of want to. I'm hurt bad."

"He gored you in two places. Don't know much about such things but I reckon Mrs. Madden can fix you up all right," Tom replied, and, turning his head, threw a long look across the flats and low hills toward the Madden ranch. Someone should be coming by then, it seemed to him.

"We've been friends for quite a spell, ain't we, Tom?"

"About three years now," Laverty replied, bringing his attention back to the stricken man.

The pad in Pettibone's chest wound was soaked and blood was beginning to seep from it. Reaching down, Tom untied the scarf encircling Henry's neck and pulled it loose.

"Got to use this," he said, snapping the cloth smartly to remove any dust. "We're a mite short of stuff for bandages."

Removing the soaked pad, he folded the neckerchief and placed it in the wound. If Mrs. Madden and the wagon didn't return soon, he guessed it would be smart to remove his shirt and rip it into strips; the bleeding had to be stopped somehow.

"Reckon I'm done for—"

"Now, don't go pulling the blanket over your head

10

yet," Tom scolded. "We've got the bleeding slowed and the wagon'll be showing up pretty soon."

"Never did like popping steers out of the brush," Pettibone said. "Sure the worst job a man can get himself into."

"You're right there," Tom said.

About twenty-five years of age, Tom was a muscular, well-built man, six feet or so in height and weighing a constant hundred and seventy pounds. With dark hair, gray eyes and a somewhat large mouth set in a square face, he was not a handsome man but rather one who gave the appearance of ruggedness and strength. Wearing usual range clothing—denim pants, faded slate-color shirt, weathered black leather vest, scarred boots, and brown, flat-crowned plainsman-style hat—he looked little different from other cowhands.

"My horse—he get away?"

Tom nodded. "Still running, I reckon. No sign of him around here. Probably lined out for the ranch."

"Yeh, prob'ly . . . Ain't them buzzards sailing around up there in the sky?"

Tom glanced skyward. A dozen or more of the big scavenger birds were circling effortlessly in broad circles against the clean, brilliant blue.

"Yesh, must have spotted something down along the river."

"Could be me—"

"Misdoubt that," Tom said, frowning. He wished Mrs. Madden and the wagon would get there. Like all ranchers' wives she was a pretty fair doctor and nurse, and would know what to do for Henry besides stanch the flow of blood from his wounds. "No, they've spotted something a couple of miles down the river . . . Best you quit talking so much."

Pettibone frowned. "That don't matter. There's some things that've got to be said before it's too late."

"Except they can wait till we get back to the ranch and Mrs. Madden's got you all doctored up."

Pettibone sighed heavily. The pad in his chest wound was beginning to look soaked again, and the entire front of his shirt was dark with blood.

"You never done no prying when we first met and started working together, Tom. I'm obliged to you for that."

Laverty's wide shoulders stirred. He again glanced off toward the Madden ranch. There was no one in sight. "Figured if there was anything you wanted me to know, you'd tell me."

Pettibone smiled faintly. "You people out in this part of the country have a good way of looking at things. Back home there would've been a lot of questions asked if a newcomer like me just blew in."

"Reckon folks just sort of look at things differently . . . You want a drink of water? Ain't got anything stronger."

Pettibone nodded slightly. "Am sort of dry."

Laverty fetched his canteen, raised Henry's head slightly, and held the container to the man's thin lips. After a couple of swallows Henry turned away.

"I'm obliged to you, Tom," he said slowly. "You

always were kind to me. I come here greener 'n grass when it come to punching cattle, and you took right to me, showed me the ropes. Weren't like the others— always guying me and playing jokes on me. I sure did appreciate it."

"Hell, Henry, every man has to start somewhere sometime. And the rest of the boys didn't mean no harm. They just like funning a new man."

"Know that, and if I don't get the chance to tell them, I want you to say I took it all kindly and never did hold no grudge."

"Sure, but you can tell them that yourself."

"Maybe. I ain't so sure. I'm feeling kind of cold inside. But I am beholden to you, and to them. I want everybody to know that."

Back in the nearby brush some small animal, a field mouse or perhaps a ground squirrel, set up a rustling noise. Overhead the buzzards continued their circling, now somewhat lower.

Pettibone reached out, laid a trembling hand on Laverty's arm. "Tom—"

"Yeh?"

"Got something I need to say to you."

2

C AN I have another swallow of that water?" Pettibone said, his words labored. "Sure mighty dry."

Laverty held the canteen to the man's lips once

more, and again threw a glance in the general direction of the Madden ranch. If the wagon didn't come soon—

Henry pushed the canteen away. He managed a weak smile. "Was plenty dry," he muttered.

Laverty shook his head. "You're doing too damn much talking. Now, I want you to hush and—"

"There ain't no time left for that, Tom . . . Reckon you didn't know I was a preacher."

"Preacher!" Laverty echoed. "Nope, I sure never figured you for that."

"Well, I was," Pettibone said. "Back in Wayne County, in Tennessee—that's where I'm from. Done some drifting around before I showed up here." Henry paused. "After my wife died it took me a spell to climb back up into the world."

Laverty shook his head, finding himself at a loss as to what he should say. He gave a side look at the dead steer. Blowflies were beginning to collect on the longhorn's bloody head.

"Mighty sorry about your wife," he murmured.

"Right then's when I turned away from God. My faith just wasn't strong enough to understand why she had to die. Good woman—a fine woman and mother."

Tom frowned. "You got some children somewhere?"

"Daughter. Name's Louanne—called her after my wife and me. Wife's name was Anne, my middle name's Louis. She's what I want to talk to you about."

Pettibone brushed at his eyes. "Louanne run off

when she was about sixteen—some four years or so ago. Was her going that killed my wife—all the worry and grief. Louanne always was a sort of restless child, and maybe too wise for her years. We done the best we could to understand her, but I reckon we failed—else she wouldn't've run off."

"You ever hear from her?"

"Yeh, she wrote a couple of times the first year telling us she was all right and for us not to fret. Said she'd found herself a good job—up in New Mexico Territory. We would have pulled stakes and moved up to be with her so's we would all be together again. I guess she figured that's just what we'd do because she told us flat out in a letter not to come. She had her own life to live, she said, and that's what she aimed to do."

Pettibone sighed wearily and fell silent. His eyes closed. Tom studied him worriedly for several moments and was about to shake him gently when Henry's lids opened.

"Can remember how we used to go up the Tennessee River—it wasn't far from the town where we lived—and fish. We had good times, Anne, Louanne, and me. We didn't have much, a team and buggy, some clothes. Me being the minister, the neighbors were always real good to us, bringing over vittles or something for Anne or Louanne to wear that they didn't want any longer. Was what you might call a comfortable life. Like I said, we didn't have much, but then we didn't want much . . . Tom, are them buzzards getting closer?"

Laverty looked upward. The big birds had dropped lower but were still well to the south.

"Yeh, seems they have but they're nowhere near us. Still off to the south."

"You for certain of that? You wouldn't go off and leave me laying here, would you, Tom?"

"Hell, Henry, you know me better than that! I'm seeing that you get back to the ranch where they'll patch you up, good as new, soon as that wagon gets here. I'm betting you'll be up riding herd in no more 'n two weeks!"

Pettibone's long fingers closed about Laverty's wrist. "You don't have to say things like that to me, Tom. I know I'm done for, and I ain't regretting it too much. I'm sorry I turned my back on God, and I've told him so aplenty of times. I reckon I'm all square with Him. What's ragging my mind now is the favor I want to ask of you."

"Sure do anything you ask if I can, Henry."

"Reach inside my shirt. Got a little pouch hanging around my neck from a rawhide string. Just skin it over my head."

Tom removed the leather pouch, not much larger than a Bull Durham tobacco sack, and placed it in Pettibone's trembling hands.

"This here's about all I've got left of the years in Tennessee—of my whole life, in fact," Henry said. "Four double eagles and a cameo necklace that come down through my wife's family. It was to go to Louanne when she got married but her running away

16

fixed that. It's a real valuable piece of jewelry we've been told, but I wouldn't know about that. Never took much stock in such things, was too busy preaching and trying to make a living for my wife and daughter.

"I want Louanne to have the cameo; it was her ma's dying wish, and now it's mine, too. That's the favor I'm asking, Tom—that you find her and give it to her. Know that's a mighty big favor to put on you but I sure would like to think Louanne would have her great-grandma's necklace, like she's supposed to, before I cash in. It ain't much of an inheritance but it's rightfully hers."

Laverty brushed at his jaw as he considered the pouch. "But if you don't know where she is, how—"

"Only thing she said was that she was working in a town near a fort, up in New Mexico. Fort Union it was. Said the town was a half-dozen miles or so away, a real pretty place right on a river. Never mentioned its name, but having the name of the fort ought to make it easy for you."

"What if she's not there? Your daughter could've moved on, and if she has, what'll I do with the cameo and the money?"

Pettibone considered that in silence. His voice had grown steadily weaker, and Tom had all but given up on the wagon and Mrs. Madden getting there in time to be of help.

"Expect I'll just have to leave that up to you. If nobody there can't tell you where she went, then the only thing you can do is keep it all for yourself. You can use the money to sort of pay your expenses if you have to keep looking for Louanne. Far as the necklace goes, if you don't ever find her, why, maybe you'll have a wife someday and you can give it to her. Can say it's a wedding present from me."

Laverty remained quiet for a time. Then, "How long since you heard from Louanne?"

"Was about two years ago—"

"Plenty could've happened in two years, Henry."

"Realize that, but I'm hoping you'll at least try to find her. Like for her to know her ma's dead—and that I'm dead, too."

"You're not dead yet! If that damn wagon—"

"I'll be gone by the time it gets here, Tom, and if I ain't, I'd never live to get back to the ranch. Got that feeling; everything's gone sort of quiet and peaceful inside me; and I ain't worrying now about anything other 'n the hope you'll do what I asked."

Pettibone became silent, his vacant eyes staring up into the blue overhead. "What I'm meaning is that you'll find Louanne and get that necklace to her. She ought to have something to remember her ma by— me, too. There's pictures of us when we got married inside it. Far as the money goes, you use it if you need to."

"I'll make out," Tom said. "Belongs to your daughter same as the cameo does."

Pettibone raised his head slightly, his eyes now bright. "You ain't said yet you'd do it."

"Never said no, either. Sure, I'll try to find her."

"She's probably working in a store—was always real good at arithmetic and figuring. Maybe she turned out to be a schoolteacher, I just can't say. Whatever, I reckon there'll be some folks in that town that'll know her, or can tell you where she went if she's gone . . . Mind staking me to another swallow of that water?"

Laverty procured the canteen, waited while Pettibone slaked his thirst. When the older man had finished, he set the cloth-covered metal container aside and turned his attention again to Henry's wounds. The one in Pettibone's side was no longer bleeding, and the one in his chest had all but stopped. It was as if Henry Pettibone's body was running out of blood.

"Tom, want to say this before I go," Pettibone said. His words were now slurred, halting, and almost inaudible. "It's been a pleasure knowing you. The way it is some men just sort of live from day to day, but—but you, you're one of the few I've known who appreciate the life the Lord gave you. You see beauty in the hills, in the creeks—in the sky and everything else—even in the grass that grows on the flats and slopes, not to mention the flowers that light up the country in the spring and summer. If—"

"You're talking too much, Henry. Lay back and rest. I can hear the wagon coming."

"I expect I'm making you kind of red-faced saying the things about you that I am, but they're the truth . . . Yeh, I can hear the wagon. Must be close."

"It'll be here in a couple of minutes. Just you hang on a bit longer."

"Aim to try, but if I'm not here when it comes, you thank the boys for me and tell them I said so long."

"Can tell them yourself, Henry," Laverty said, and, rising to his feet, beckoned impatiently to the men on the seat of the approaching vehicle. He swore softly. Mrs. Madden was not with them. Henry would have to wait awhile longer for her good medical attention.

"Over here!" he yelled, waving his arms.

He knew the men in the wagon could see him; the dead longhorn was sufficient marker, but pent-up anger and frustration over the length of time it had taken for help to arrive was tearing him apart.

"Pull up over here!" he shouted once more as the vehicle swerved to avoid the steer. "Where the hell have you been?"

"Come fast as we could, Tom," the driver said. "Had to hitch up the team, and we waited a bit hoping Mrs. Madden would get back from town so's she could come along. Jeremiah finally told us we'd better go on without her."

"How bad hurt is he?" the other man on the seat asked after he'd dropped to the ground.

Tom crouched beside Pettibone. In the hard, driving sunlight the man's features were slack and as white as the alkali flats south of the ranch. His eyes were half closed and the faint hint of a contented smile parted his thin lips. Tom reached out, searched Henry's wrist for a pulse. There was none.

"Pettibone's dead," he said in reply.

The driver of the wagon, a grizzled, bearded oldster

known as Navy, shrugged. "Well, I reckon that's about as hurt as a man can get. Come on, let's load him in the wagon and get started back. Getting on to dinner time."

3

FUNERAL services for Henry Pettibone were held late that afternoon at the family burial plot a quarter mile or so from the ranch. It was a quiet, tree-shaded place separated from the surrounding land by a whitewashed picket fence and cheered by numerous flowers and bushes planted and cultivated by Jeremiah Madden's wife Caroline.

The cemetery was divided into two sections. The east end contained the remains of the two Madden children, killed in a runaway accident when they were small; the remaining half, on the west side, was reserved for the ranch hands who died or were killed while working for the Maddens, and had no other home. There were five oblong mounds with wooden markers there, Laverty noticed during the brief ceremony conducted by Jeremiah Madden. Henry Louis Pettibone would make the sixth.

"He was a fine man," the rancher said to Tom as they walked slowly back to the ranch house. "Henry was a close friend of yours, I know, and I reckon you'll miss him for a spell."

Tom nodded. "Will for sure. I need to talk to you for a bit, Jeremiah. I made a promise to Henry before he died."

"That so?" Madden said, pausing to glance out over his south range. Far to the right a small herd of a hundred or so steers was drifting across a grassy swale toward a cluster of trees where there was a water hole.

"I'm going to have to quit," Laverty said bluntly.

Madden came about quickly, a deep frown on his face. In his sixties, he was a tall, lean, gray-looking individual who had been a cowman all his adult life.

"Quit? Hell, Tom, there ain't no reason to quit."

"Maybe not, but I promised Henry I'd track down his daughter and give her some family things he wanted her to have."

"Family? I didn't even know he was a married man!" Madden said, surprised. "Any idea where his daughter is—and what about his wife?"

"She's dead. Daughter's up in New Mexico somewhere—a town close to a fort."

"Several forts in New Mexico. Know which one?"

"Union."

Madden nodded. Back in the trees surrounding the small cemetery a dove was calling softly into the fading day.

"Fort Union's a far piece from here," the rancher said after a time. "It'll take you a couple of weeks at least to make the ride."

"Figured to be gone a spell, and I thought long as I was up there I'd go on to Wyoming. Always had a hankering to see that part of the country—specially Cheyenne."

Madden's shoulders stirred. "You're talking about

being gone for a couple of months, maybe all summer."

Tom nodded. "That's about the size of it."

"It's a bad time of the year to have you gone, but I expect I can find somebody to hire on. Plenty of drifters looking for work. Means I'll need to replace you as well as Pettibone. Don't mind saying it'll be hard to do; you're one of my best hands. Goes for Pettibone, too."

"Sure hate to put you in a bind. Like working here, but I gave Henry my word and—"

"I'm not about to ask you to break it, either," Madden said as they moved on.

Most of the remaining hands had reached the hard-pack and were heading for the bunkhouse. Smoke was twisting up from the stovepipe chimney of the kitchen into the bronze-looking glare of sunset, and the cook would soon be hammering the bit of iron that hung outside the cook shack door, summoning the help to supper.

"You aiming to stay up in Wyoming once you get there?"

At Madden's question Laverty shrugged. "Sure don't know. Always heard it was real pretty country in the summer but plain hell in the winter. Kind of like to find out for myself."

"Heard that, too. Winters there are hard on cattle, horses, and man, but I know telling you that's not enough. Best you find out for yourself."

"Yeh, reckon so."

"Well, Tom, you go ahead, but keep this in mind: this here's the only good part of the country for a man to live in. You'll learn that once you're gone. Now, you go right ahead with your plans; then, when you get tired of ass-deep snow and wind that can cut a man in two, come on back here. There'll be a job waiting for you."

Laverty grinned, thrust out his hand, and as the rancher took it into his own, said: "You're a real fair man, Jeremiah. And I expect you can look for me coming back someday; and that'll be just as soon as I can get Cheyenne and Wyoming out of my blood."

"I'll be looking for you," Madden said. "Now draw your rations from the cook and pick yourself a pack-horse. You're going to find there's plenty of open country between here and there, and you'll need to carry plenty of grub, feed for your animals, and water . . . You won't be forgetting to say good-bye to the missus, will you? She sets great store by you."

"No sir, I won't forget. Have to tell the rest of the crew, too. Haven't said anything to anybody about what I aimed to do. Wanted to talk to you first."

"I appreciate that. When are you fixing to pull out?"

"Tomorrow morning—if it's all right with you."

"Good a time as any. I'll say so long now, and lots of luck."

"Obliged to you, Jeremiah," Laverty said, nodding. "And the same to you."

Tom rode out that next morning shortly before first

light after weathering much advice and joshing from the rest of Madden's hired hands. He had accepted the rancher's advice and was taking along a packhorse, a tough, close-coupled little buckskin, although he would have preferred not to. Such horses slowed a man down considerably, and he was anxious to reach Fort Union and the town nearby, where he hoped to find Louanne Pettibone, and there discharge his obligation to Henry. After that he could continue on to Cheyenne.

Leaving the Madden Ranch, Tom followed the San Pedro north until he reached a point beyond the Galiuro Mountains where Aravaipa Creek entered the river, and there began to bear northeast. He continued on in that direction, skirting the White Mountain area and ending up finally at a lumber town called Springerville.

He encountered no trouble during the first leg of the journey although he did encounter several small parties of Indians, none of whom was either friendly or hostile but who simply watched him pass in wary silence.

Tom rested the horses for a day in Springerville, whiling the time away in one of the several saloons and gambling houses, and then moved on—feeling the bite of the high, cold mountainous country, which evoked thoughts of the warm San Pedro. But that was but a fleeting half regret and he gave it no more consideration as he crossed over into New Mexico, followed a well-marked trail through the Mogollon

Mountains that led him on to the San Augustine Plains and eventually to Socorro, a fair-sized town on the Rio Grande.

He stocked up at a general store there, buying grub for himself and grain for the horses.

"How far you going?" the storekeeper asked in a friendly voice.

"Fort Union," Tom replied, taking no offense.

The merchant whistled softly. "Long ways from here!"

"How many days?"

"Ten, maybe eleven—or twelve. Pretty hard going in places, specially where you climb up into the mountains and get onto the high plains country."

Laverty sighed. It seemed he had already been in the saddle for weeks instead of only a few days, and he apparently still had a long way to go. But he reckoned it wouldn't be so bad; he had seen a lot of new country, and now he would see more.

"Just follow the river north," the storekeeper said when Laverty was ready to move out. "It'll be easier traveling. A lot cooler, too. When you get up close to Santa Fe, you'll have to cut east and either cut through the Sangre de Cristos—that's the mountain range up there—or circle around their south end."

"Which'll be easiest—and fastest?"

"Well, I'd circle around the end. There's some mighty steep climbing if you try cutting across to Fort Union, and you're sure to run into snow. The south road's a good one. Take you right to Las Vegas. Once you're there, you're about thirty miles from the fort."

Traveling along the Rio Grande was pleasant. The trail was open, giant cottonwood trees, willows, and other shrubs grew along its banks, and the ground was covered with a thick grass. Birds seemed to be everywhere, and now and then he startled a grazing deer or some small animal in his passage.

There were many small farms, and as he rode by, the men and women working in the fields paused to wave a friendly greeting. He came to an Indian village and, wary of any hostility, passed it by at a distance, aware that a dozen or more of the men, lined up against the wall of one of the mud-plastered huts, watched him ride by with sullen interest.

On north of the small, bleak village, the valley's green beauty continued, and as he rode along the river's bank that next day with towering mountains to the east and the dormant cones of several volcanoes on the west, Tom wondered if his journey would continue under such pleasant circumstances.

Matters changed but little, he learned, as he pressed steadily on, occasionally encountering other pilgrims, passing through several more small settlements and Indian villages until finally the trail began to swing away from the river and climb out onto an almost barren, rock-bound plain. The area was devoid of any growth other than cactus, sharp-pointed yucca plants, and low brush. Laverty found little else to wonder at for the remainder of the way to Santa Fe.

He laid over there in the old Spanish capital for a

day and then, anxious to reach Fort Union—and recalling the advice of the Socorro storekeeper—took the road that circled the base of the snowcapped Sangre de Cristos and led to the next town of size, Las Vegas.

Arriving in that settlement two days later, Tom realized he was not too far from his destination, a thought that filled him with considerable cheer as he drew up to the hitch rack of a fairly large building bearing the sign THE MEADOW CITY SALOON across its front. He'd treat himself to a couple of drinks, find a restaurant, and after having a meal, ride on. In another day or two the long ride would be over insofar as his promise to Henry Pettibone was concerned—and assuming his old friend's daughter would be in the town where she was said to be.

But the journey was only about half finished if he still intended to see Cheyenne. He reckoned he'd have to mull that about in his head a bit; accustomed as he was to the saddle, he was sore and bone weary of the hard leather hull, and once he got to that town where Louanne Pettibone lived and settled with her, he'd rent himself a room in a hotel and take it easy for at least a week while he got the bow out of his legs. He'd decide then if he'd continue on to Wyoming, stay right where he was for a time, or head back south for the San Pedro and Jeremiah Madden's ranch.

Shortly before noon that next day Tom reached a small village north of Las Vegas and halted at its general store. As he entered, a squat, balding man wearing a denim apron over a rumpled gray shirt and baggy brown pants came forward to greet him.

"Howdy. Name's Davidson. What can I do for you?"

"Need a couple a' sacks of Bull Durham," Laverty replied, and as the merchant stepped in behind a glass-fronted case to get the items, added: "Mind telling me where I am? Didn't see any signs anywhere."

Davidson paused, looked at Tom closely. "Brother, you sure must've had a hard night!"

Laverty shrugged. "Nope, not that. Just happen to be a stranger."

Davidson nodded and said, "I see. Well, the town's name is Watrous. It used to be called La Junta and lots of folks still call it that. You're at the fork in the Santa Fe Trail, where the Cutoff begins. Where're you headed?"

"Guess I'd say Fort Union only I—"

"If you're going there, just take the road that leads off to the left when you leave town. Goes right to the fort. Can't miss it because you can see it soon as you're over that rise. Besides, you'll see soldiers out there on the flats . . . Anything else you need besides this tobacco?"

"Nope, that's all. The fort's not exactly where I want to go. I'm looking for a town on a river somewhere nearby. Have to find the daughter of a friend of mine. Happen to know the name of it, and where it is?"

Davidson dropped the two sacks of cigarette makings on the counter and brushed at the stubble of whiskers on his jaw.

"Sure I know—same as everybody else around these parts knows. Place is called Sodom on the Mora."

4

"S ODOM on the Mora!" Laverty echoed. "What the hell kind of a name is that for a town?"

Davidson pushed the tobacco and papers toward Tom. "Not its real name, of course. Loma Parda, that's what it's supposed to be called. Most of us just say Pardo . . . You owe me twenty cents."

Laverty handed over the specified change and picked up his purchase. "Sodom on the Mora," he murmured. "How did it ever get a name like that?"

The storekeeper took a blackened briar pipe from a shelf, glanced at the contents in its bowl, and thrust the stem between his teeth. Striking a match, he held the flame over the charred opening of the pipe and puffed the tobacco within it into life. Expelling a cloud of smoke, he considered Laverty.

"Can't rightly answer that. Was what folks were calling it when I come here a few years back, but I expect it was some wag who knew a little about the Bible that gave it that name. The town sets right on the Mora River."

Tom nodded. "I'm beginning to understand. It's a real wild, wide-open place, that it?"

"Well, every fort has a hell-town. Sodom's Fort Union's. Don't mean no disrespect, but if that friend of yours has a daughter living there, why—"

Davidson broke off, and fell silent. Out behind the store chickens were clucking in a pen as they scratched about in the loose dust.

"Sure don't seem like the place my friend was talking about," Tom admitted. "Expect I've made a mistake, but I'll have to go there and find out for certain."

"Can see that. Best you watch your step, however. The town's full of cutthroats, thieves, gamblers, and wicked women who'd as soon kill a man as look at him. Same goes for a lot of the soldiers from the fort. They're plenty mean."

"Ain't there no law there?"

"Got a town marshal by the name of Zack Fish, but he ain't much. Just don't have no power, mainly because the saloon owners and most of the storekeepers don't want any law. They like things just the way they are. Truth is the Army's the only one that can do anything."

"I'd think they'd step in and take a hand if things are as bad as you say."

"They do—on a kind of a regular basis. Every time they change the fort commander, the new man tries to do something about it. Heard it said that when Colonel Kit Carson was running Union, matters did get some better, but even he was never able to really clean up the town."

Davidson paused to knock the dottle from his pipe. "You got to remember," he continued as he refilled the old briar from a leather pouch, "that at one time they

31

had near three thousand soldiers stationed there. Was during the Civil War. Town was really a wild one then. Could figure on a killing or two every night, and even the U.S. marshals stayed clear of it.

"There was a major that took over after Carson was gone. Name I think was Johnson, or maybe it was Thompson. Anyway, he swore he was going to clean up the place, make it a decent and safe place for soldiers to go and spend their time and money."

On the road passing in front of Davidson's, two canvas-topped wagons rumbled by, wheels creaking, chains rattling, the worn, sunburned faces of their occupants turned toward the store in lethargic contemplation.

"The major didn't have any better luck than the commanders ahead of him," Davidson continued. "He tried his best, I reckon, but the town just naturally wouldn't cooperate. They wanted the soldiers to be spending their time and hard cash there, and while they was always sorry about the killings and done their best to keep such things from happening, they just never got nowhere."

"You think you might know my friend's daughter if she's working there? Could be she's done some trading with you."

"Doubt it," Davidson said. "Women there don't get out of the town hardly. Fact is, it's pretty much like being in the pen for them. What's this here girl's name?"

"Pettibone—Louanne Pettibone."

The merchant shook his head. "Nope, sure never heard of her, but I've only been over there a couple of times in my life—and my wife don't know about that."

"Expect there's a lot of women—"

"Quite a few, all right. Besides John King's place—he calls it King's Castle—there's at least a dozen more brothels and saloons. King's is the biggest and most popular, and he more or less runs the town."

"Expect he's the man for me to talk to."

"Maybe, but was it me looking for somebody, I'd ask Zack Fish. If she's working there in Pardo—that's the town's real name—he'll know her."

"Her pa figured she would be working in a store of some kind, maybe a dressmaker's shop, or that she might even be a schoolteacher. Can't figure his daughter being a saloon woman, knowing him like I did."

"Not much chance of that," Davidson said in his flat, nasal voice. "Only a few stores there and they're run by men. And a schoolteacher? Well, there ain't any school. Decent folks with children won't live there."

Laverty shrugged and glanced again to the street. More wagons headed west were rolling by. The occupants were usually a bearded man, a sunbonneted woman on the seat, and several round-faced children peering out from beneath the canvas top of the vehicle—all with the steadfast hope of better things to come in their hearts.

"Probably all going to California," Davidson said, his eyes also on the pilgrims, "but like as not they'll never get there. The wagons'll break down, or some of the party will get sick, and they'll have to stop—and that's where they'll settle. If they're lucky it'll be near water, and there won't be any hostile Indians around."

"There many of them in this country?"

"Still a few; that's why they keep the fort open. Have to be on the lookout for raiding parties, renegades mostly, all the time. Just the other day—"

"Expect I'd better get over to Pardo and start asking around for Louanne," Tom broke in. He'd heard all he wanted to about that part of the country and the fort and was anxious to find out where things stood with Henry Pettibone's daughter.

"Best you go careful. King and the others like him don't cotton much to somebody nosing around. And there's aplenty of men hiding from the law there in Pardo—probably more than's running loose in the whole territory!"

"Not hard to believe . . . This road that goes to the fort, it go to the town, too?"

"Not exactly," Davidson said. "Stay on it till you come to the river. Then follow the trail that runs alongside. Soon as you come to the bridge, cross it—and you'll be there."

Laverty reached for the merchant's hand and shook it. "I'm obliged to you for telling me what you did. Expect I'll be seeing you again."

"Sure hope so," the storekeeper said. "Just you

watch your *P*s and *Q*s and maybe you'll get out of there alive."

"Aim to do just that."

"And don't back off of using that gun you're carrying if you need to. Good luck."

"Looks like I'll be needing plenty of that," Tom said, and nodding to the merchant, walked to the door and stepped out into the bright sunlight.

A half-dozen blue-clad cavalrymen drew up as he stepped off the landing. All eyed him narrowly but the young lieutenant who apparently was in command of the squad smiled faintly, touched the brim of his campaign hat with a forefinger as he dismounted, and struck for Davidson's.

"Good day to you, sir," he said in a voice unmistakably Texan.

Tom bobbed. "And the same to you, Lieutenant," he replied, and mounting, rode on.

Tom was conscious of the soldiers' eyes following him as he swung onto the road leading north. No doubt they were wondering who he was and why he was in the area. Such speculation would be heightened when they saw him veer off the heavily traveled tracks to the fort onto the trail that led to Pardo.

Could he be a new lawman sent in by the territorial governor to tame the town? Was he an inspector general in disguise, there to see what the Army might do about shutting the town down?

Laverty grinned, shrugged. Let them think what they wished as long as they didn't get in his way. He was there for one purpose only—locate Louanne, hand over her legacy, and ride on—but he was still finding it difficult to believe he'd find Henry Pettibone's daughter in a wild hell-town like Sodom on the Mora.

5

L AVERTY stared out over the plain to the distant collection of structures that was Fort Union. With no wall surrounding it, as might be expected, it lay in the center of a broad swale, clearly out in the open as if defying any hostile force to challenge it. He could see figures moving about on what was apparently the parade ground. Further over, a platoon of cavalrymen was moving briskly eastward from the fortification in the direction of the Santa Fe Trail, either in a maneuver or in response to some emergency.

Far to the left Tom could see the towering Sangre de Cristo Mountains, their higher peaks glistening with snow despite the warmth of late May. The slopes of the nearby hills were blanketed with bright flowers—yellow columbine and blue flax—while along the Mora River, which proved to be hardly more than a creek at that point, he recognized larkspur and the tightly closed blossoms of evening primrose.

The ground was covered with grass and trees grew along the stream. On upstream he could see smoke rising from a canyon on its far side and reckoned that would mark the location of Pardo, the town with the unsavory nickname.

As he crossed the narrow wooden bridge a short distance on, the sound of gunshots coming from the settlement reached him, and the thought of what storekeeper Davidson had said about the place came to mind. It all boiled down to one thing: he had best watch his step.

Laverty smiled tightly. He aimed to do exactly that; and he'd stay in Pardo no longer than was necessary. He still had doubts that Louanne Pettibone could be found in such a town, but Pardo fit the location Henry had given him, which made it pretty certain. Likely she had been there when she wrote the letter to him, but subsequently finding the place not suitable to her liking, moved on.

Laverty reached the edge of the settlement and drew to a halt. Two dozen or more soldiers were moving about on what might be considered a street along which were arranged in irregular fashion the saloons, brothels, and other business houses. King's Castle was the most prominent of all. A fairly large frame and rock structure with a pitched roof, it dominated the area. Beyond it close by were several small huts, probably occupied or used by the women who worked the saloon, Tom guessed.

On down the street he could see other saloons: the Paris, the Black Eagle, the Cavalryman, the Yellow Rose, several that appeared nameless but all offering liquor, gambling, girls, and rooms to let. Laverty could see a livery stable, two or three stores, and a few more unidentified buildings. A number of houses were visible in the canyon, all set along the Mora River, which wound its way through the tall grass and cottonwood trees that flourished on its banks.

Two men suddenly burst through the open doorway of King's Castle and stumbled into the center of the street. Not in soldiers' uniforms, but in ordinary range clothing, they were locked in tight embrace as each sought to wrestle the other to the dusty ground. Three onlookers followed them into the open, and several soldiers loafing in the shadow of the nearby Paris Saloon crossed over leisurely to watch, but the fight drew little attention; no doubt such brawls were common occurrences in Pardo.

A hack rolled in from the river crossing and halted in the center of the town. Doors on either side flung open and a dozen soldiers leaped out. Tom shook his head in wonder. Evidently the merchants operated a transportation service to and from the fort to make it easier for the men stationed there to partake of what Pardo had to offer.

Laverty watched the uniformed men separate, some going to King's, others heading for the Paris and the Cavalryman, or their favorite haunt along the roadway. The empty hack moved on to one of the unidentified buildings, which evidently served as a waiting room and headquarters for the transportation service.

The brawl in the street, unnoticed by the new

arrivals, came to a stop, and the two men involved as well as the bystanders disappeared into the noisy depths of the Castle. Tom glanced about for a general store. A faded sign bearing the name HAZLETT'S on a building farther along identified the merchant. He'd go there first, Laverty decided, and ask about Louanne. Failing to turn up any information, he'd locate the town marshal, as Davidson had suggested, or pay a visit to King's Castle and talk to the owner. Among the three he should find out about the girl.

Spurring his horse lightly, Tom rode on, the little buckskin following closely at the end of the lead rope attached to his halter. A soldier yelled something unintelligible as he passed but Laverty only raised a hand as if responding to a greeting. Something was going on inside one of the smaller saloons; another fight, Tom guessed, judging from the yells and the sound of furniture being smashed.

Reaching the hitch rack at the side of Hazlett's, he dismounted and secured the bay to the crossbar. There was no landing or porch fronting the store as was the usual arrangement where business houses were concerned, but only a single step. Nor was there a screen door, and Tom walked directly into the shadowy interior of the building.

"Howdy!" The voice came from the rear of the thinly stocked store.

The smell of freshly baked bread—priced at one dollar a loaf—mingling with the odors of coal oil, tobacco, leather, and other staples filled the room.

"Morning," Laverty responded, straining to adjust his eyes to the change in light. "You Hazlett?"

"That I am," said a man, standing behind a crude counter across the front of which was a red-and-white metal sign advertising chewing tobacco. "What can I do for you?"

Tom crossed to the counter. "You been around here long?"

"Going on five year," the merchant said. "Why?"

"Expect you've seen a lot of folks come and go," Laverty said, and pointed to a box of cigars. "Reckon I'll have one of those stogies."

Two soldiers came into the store. Walking up to the glass case where bread was kept, one flipped a silver dollar to the storekeeper while the other opened the case and removed one of the golden brown, cylindrical loaves. Breaking it in two, he handed half to his partner, and then, still wordless, both returned to the street.

"Seems everything's mighty dear around here," Tom said as he lit the cigar.

"Everything is," Hazlett replied, pocketing the coin Laverty had laid on the counter, "but that's egg bread—real special. It along with pies and cakes are some extra I sell. The wife does the baking, can hardly keep up with the demand. The bread in that case'll all be gone in another hour . . . There be anything else for you?"

"Not right now," Tom said. "My grub sack's getting a bit light, but I'll wait until tomorrow and then drop by so's you can stock it up. Right now I'm needing information. You know a girl, or I reckon she's a woman now, called Louanne Pettibone?"

Hazlett repeated the name. "Can't say that I do. Do know one that works for John King that calls herself Lou. Don't think I ever heard her last name. Why?"

Laverty shrugged, blew a cloud of smoke into the still, warm air. "Like to talk to her."

Hazlett's slim, dark face hardened. A tall, lean man, he had small, close-set eyes, a hawk-beak nose, and thin lips.

"You some kind of a lawman?" he asked. "If you are, you'd best get right back on your horse and—"

"I'm not a lawman," Laverty cut in. "This Louanne's the daughter of a friend of mine. He asked me to look her up."

The merchant settled back, satisfied. "Glad to hear that. I don't like to see any more trouble around here than what just turns up naturally."

"Be no trouble far as I'm concerned," Tom said. "It could be this Lou is not the woman I'm looking for. Louanne Pettibone's more likely to be a schoolteacher or a dressmaker, or a clerk in a store like this."

Another soldier entered the store, helped himself to a loaf of the still-warm bread as well as a pie. He nodded to Laverty and then to Hazlett.

"You'll have to put this on my bill, Ed. I'm busted flat till payday."

Hazlett said, "Sure," and as the private left made a notation on a slip of paper and impaled it on a spindle.

He brought his attention back to Laverty. "Murphy's one of the few I carry on account. Always pays up on time."

Tom watched the soldier disappear down the street. Then, "Don't they feed good out at that fort?"

"Oh sure, but it ain't nothing but regular army chow. Around here my wife's fresh bread's like dessert to the boys . . . But getting back to this gal you're looking for; what makes you think she'd be here?"

"Wrote her pa naming this place."

"You sure this is it?"

"Said a town right close to Fort Union. According to folks I've talked to, this'll be the place."

"She didn't give him no name?"

"Forgot to mention it, I reckon. Just sort of told him where it was."

"Hell, she probably didn't want to tell him the name. This town's sure not where any decent woman would come to live simply because there's no place for them to work other 'n saloons and bawdy houses. Pardo's here for the benefit of the soldiers, and nothing else."

"Looks like they're about all there is around," Tom said as a group of uniformed men, laughing and talking loud, passed by. "The commander out at the fort just let them come and go as they please?"

"Almost. The colonel running things out there now is pretty loose with the men. If they don't have any duty, they've got leave to come to town. Can even stay all night, long as they're there for roll call."

"Makes it pretty soft."

"Well, maybe. The post commanders haven't all been that way. Had a few in charge since I've been here that tried to enforce real strict regulations about the town. And there's been a couple or so that put the town off limits, but hell, they were just spitting into the wind. Soldiers would somehow sneak off and come anyway—which was easy to do as we're only about five miles from Union, and the town never shuts down.

"And there's no harm being done. Sure there's fights, but that goes on out behind the barracks at the fort all the time. Bound to happen when you throw a lot of men from different places together. We try to keep things leveled off much as possible, but it's pretty wild around here and we do have a killing every now and then. That's the big thing that riles the commandant out at Union—having one of his yellowlegs shot up."

"Yeh, expect it would," Laverty said, turning to leave. "Obliged to you for your time. Think I'll stable my horses, get them off the street, then go see if this woman you mentioned is the one I'm looking for."

"Expect the only way you'll know is to talk to her, all right. One thing, howsomever; walk mighty careful out there at night unless you want to use that gun you're carrying. Things on the street are quiet right now, but let it get dark and a man's life ain't worth much unless he's willing to fight for it."

Laverty smiled. "I'm obliged to you again, Hazlett," he said, and leaving the store, mounted his horse and headed for the livery stable.

Somewhere back up the street a voice shouted: *"Shoot the sonofabitch!"* That seemed to reflect the tone of life in the settlement, and the air of tension and violence that hung over it was almost palpable. But none of that need concern him, Tom thought. While he was not adverse to a little excitement and was certain he could hold his own should he by some circumstance be forced into gunplay, he preferred to avoid it. All he wanted was to find Louanne Pettibone, discharge what he considered his sworn duty to her, and move on.

6

BELLWOOD'S LIVERY BARN was a stone building with a long, slanting tin roof. It was not as large as a public stable usually is, but it was well lighted by several windows, and as Laverty rode into the runway he saw a man at work in the back on what appeared to be a coffin.

The man, a burly-looking redhead with a full mustache and beard, and dressed only in stained underwear, bib overalls, and thick-soled shoes, ceased his carpentry and came forward.

"You looking to leave your horses?" he asked in a booming voice. "I'm Ike Bellwood."

Tom swung down from the bay. "Want them both taken care of," he said. "They've come a far piece."

"Reckon I'll do the best I can. Shorthanded on hired

help right now. When'll you be riding out?"

"Tomorrow—maybe."

"All right. Just don't make it no sooner," Bellwood said, taking the reins of the bay. "You want any of your gear?"

"Later," Laverty said. "There a place in this town where a man can rent a room?"

Bellwood brushed at his thick mustache. The backs of his hands and his brawny arms were covered with large freckles. When he moved, the muscles both under and outside the soiled underwear stirred gently.

"Hell, man, pick any saloon along the street and you can rent yourself a room. A woman comes with it."

"Not the kind I'm looking for right now. Want someplace to sleep."

Bellwood shrugged his massive shoulders. "Ain't no place in this town for that. Best you go to the Adams place. It's up the canyon a ways. It's a boardinghouse but the old lady'll find a room for you."

Bellwood had separated the horses and led each into a stall, and was starting to strip the bay. Laverty, stepping in beside the buckskin, began to unload him.

"Looks like a coffin you're working on back there," he said. "You the undertaker around here, too?"

"One of them," the stableman said. "Was a killing about an hour ago. Gambler. I'm boxing him up now."

That had been the shooting he heard as he was nearing the settlement, Tom guessed.

"Town's likely in for some bad trouble when that colonel out at the fort hears about it," Bellwood said, hanging Laverty's saddle over the wall of the stall.

"Didn't you say the dead man was a gambler?"

"Yeh."

"If he wasn't a soldier, I don't see why the Army can get all worked up over it."

"There's been too many killings here—soldiers and civilians both. Wasn't long ago the colonel served notice on the town marshal and all of us in business that the next time there was a shooting he was moving in and taking things into his own hands."

"Meaning by that he'd throw the man who did the killing into his stockade and maybe stand him up before a firing squad, I suppose."

"Yes, and worse. He said he'd close the saloon where it happened and then burn it down. Got us all jumpy as a wormy horse, I'm telling you for sure!"

"Can see how it would; you can't keep your finger on every man in town."

"That's for damn sure."

"By the way, you know a woman, a young one, by the name of Louanne Pettibone? Friend of mine asked me to look her up."

Bellwood paused, ran his big hand down the bay's withers. "Pettibone? No, can't say as I do. One or two of the girls around call themselves Lou. They don't usually bother with last names. You best go ask—"

Bellwood glanced up as several riders and a man on foot appeared in the entrance of the livery stable. The mounted men were soldiers. Sunlight glinted off the star on the vest of the one walking. The stable owner swore deeply.

"Knew they'd be coming, damn it!" he muttered. "Sure didn't take them long."

"Who are they?"

"Soldiers are from the fort, sent by that colonel. The lawman is Zack Fish, the town marshal. They'll be wanting to have a look at the dead man."

"Ike, you back there?"

"Right here, the stableman said, and stepped out of the stall into the runway. "What can I do for you?"

"Got Major Kinkaid and Lieutenant Joseph here with me. The major wants a look at that gambler who got himself killed," the lawman said, his voice reflecting his irritation. "Expect he wants to be sure it wasn't one of his soldier boys."

"Well, he sure ain't!" Bellwood said as the three men headed on down the runway. "Come right on back here, Major and have a look. I was just getting him all boxed up for burying. If you'da come a few minutes later, you'd been too late."

"And if you'd had that coffin nailed shut, you would have had to open it up," the officer, a thin, sharp-faced, peacock kind of a man, said sharply.

Bellwood started to make a reply, and then thought better of it. "Sure, sure," he murmured as he continued to lead the way to the wooden coffin.

Tom felt the junior officer's eyes upon him, curious and thoughtful. In the next moment he recognized the lieutenant who had spoken to him as he was leaving Davidson's store earlier in the day. Laverty nodded, and Joseph responded similarly.

"Here's your dead man," Bellwood said, halting beside the crude coffin. "Can see with your own eyes he ain't one of your soldier boys."

Kinkaid glanced down at the slack features of the gambler, and then at the garish black-and-yellow-checked suit, red vest, and frilled white shirt. The vest and shirt had been unbuttoned where someone had tried to get to the wound in the man's chest and render aid. Evidently it had been in vain; the bullet had apparently gone straight into the heart.

"Name?" the major asked curtly.

"Somebody said he was called Deaver—Jake Deaver," the harried-looking lawman replied.

A man somewhere in his forties, Laverty supposed, Zack Fish was short, husky, had but little hair and pale blue eyes. He wore a dark blue army-style shirt, tan leather vest, dark pants, knee-high boots, and a brown, narrow-brimmed hat. A bone-handled Colt hung at his right hip, and he carried a double-barrel shotgun in the crook of his left arm.

Kinkaid gave that thought, and then shrugged. "Make a note of that, Lieutenant. The colonel will want full particulars concerning the man's identity; also some verification."

Joseph nodded. "Yes, sir, I'll get right on it."

"Ain't much to verify," Bellwood said, picking up the lid of the coffin and sliding it into place. "Man was a gambler and he's dead. You think maybe he was one of your soldier boys and I switched clothes on him?"

"Not thinking anything, mister!" Kinkaid snapped. "Point is the colonel wants facts and it's my job to see that he gets them." The officer turned abruptly to Laverty, now standing in the runway. "You have something to do with this? You the man who killed him?"

Tom felt anger stir at the officer's brusque attitude, but before he could reply Bellwood spoke up.

"Nope, wasn't him. I seen him ride in a little bit after the shooting took place."

Kinkaid's nose curled. "Just what this town needs: another outlaw gunfighter."

"You don't know that, Major," Bellwood said, raising his hand to restrain Laverty. "Come here looking for somebody. If he don't find her, expect he'll keep moving on."

The major's hard-set features altered little. "Maybe. You got a name, mister?"

"Yeh, I've got a name," Laverty said coldly. "It's Tom Laverty—and it's mister to you."

Kinkaid smiled dryly. "All right, Mr. Tom Laverty, best thing you can do is keep riding," he said, and turned back to Bellwood. "Who was it then that did the shooting?"

"Sure can't tell you that, Major. Best you go over to the Paris and ask around. Maybe you'll get somebody to talk."

"I doubt that," Kinkaid said. "Nobody around here ever knows anything about a killing. The whole damn town seems to be deaf, dumb, and blind at such times . . . Lieutenant, hadn't you better be about your business?"

"Yes, sir," Joseph replied, and snapping a quick salute, spun on a heel and returned to the waiting cavalrymen, still in their saddles at the entrance to the livery barn.

Bellwood, signifying the interview was over as far as he was concerned, picked up a handful of nails and a hammer and began to nail down the lid on Jake Deaver's coffin. The officer watched in silence for several moments and then, turning, headed for the door. Fish, a half smile on his thin lips, came about and followed.

When they had reached the wide front entrance and disappeared into the street, Laverty moved up closer. "Obliged to you for speaking up for me," he said. "That major's a bit on the hard-nosed side. Doubt if he'd believe anything I told him."

"Kinkaid's the kind that believes what he wants to believe," Bellwood said, driving a final nail into the coffin's lid. He gave Tom a side glance. "What I said was right, wasn't it? You did ride in after the shooting—"

Laverty grinned. "Fact is I did. Heard the shots just before I reached town."

"Well, I reckon it don't make much difference. I just didn't want to give that popinjay the satisfaction of thinking he'd come onto something . . . Who was it you said you'd come here for?"

"Woman named Pettibone. She's the daughter of a

friend of mine that just got himself killed. Steer gored him. Before he died he asked me to look her up and—"

"Yeh, well I sure can't help you none, Tom. Never have heard of no Louannes around here. Couple of Lous, and I ain't never heard the name Pettibone. One of them Lous might be the woman you're looking for."

"There's a chance. Henry—that's the name of her pa—said I'd find her here."

"Well, if you do, she won't be no lily-white lady like you're maybe expecting, just you better make up your mind to that. Now, was I the one looking for somebody wearing a skirt, I'd start at the Castle. That's the place where you'll find the most women."

"I see . . . How much do I owe you? Like to pay you now."

"If you're riding out tomorrow, it'll be three dollars."

"Not sure yet about that," Laverty said, handing over the necessary amount. "All depends."

"Well, if she ain't at the Castle," Bellwood said, pocketing the coins, "I expect one of the girls there can tell you where she is—if she was ever here."

Tom nodded, and turned toward the door. "Like as not I'll drop by later."

"Fair enough but just don't change your mind about riding out and finding your horses ready. I've got to lug this coffin out to the boneyard and plant it—if Old Man Ortega's through digging the hole."

"Not much chance of me needing them before

tomorrow," Tom said, and continued along the runway.

7
___

A LATE afternoon coolness had set in, turning the air in the high plains country brisk as Laverty entered the street and bent his steps for King's Castle. He had decided earlier to seek Louanne Pettibone there first, and should he have no success, go then to see town marshal Zack Fish as someone had suggested.

More soldiers were to be seen now, and taking note, Tom reckoned he was the only man about not in uniform. A wagon loaded with a half-dozen additional patrons-to-be from the fort rolled in, its spinning wheels stirring up clouds of powdery dust as it headed for the row of unnamed buildings. But the men crouched in the vehicle's narrow bed did not wait for it to reach the depot. Yelling, laughing, and cursing, they abandoned it while it was still in motion and, scattering like chickens before a coyote, hurried to their favored saloon.

There was a small landing fronting King's, and stepping up onto it, Laverty crossed to the open doorway. A blast of sound and a mixture of odors met him head-on as he entered the building, and the thought came to him that if King's Castle was this active in daylight hours, what would it be like at night?

An argument was taking place between two

cowhands standing just inside the door, and Tom, stepping to one side to avoid the big-hatted, spurred, and well-armed pair, backed up against the wall for a good look at the saloon's teeming interior.

The place was large and well lighted by several large chandeliers hanging by ropes from the rafters of the ceilingless structure. Lamps also were bracketed on the walls, which were adorned with calendars, glassy-eyed deer heads, and paintings of voluptuous nude women in various poses. A piano, barely audible above the din, was being played in a far corner where an area had been fenced off for dancing. Several couples were within the railed section, rocking back and forth or stomping vigorously to the sound of the music.

The bar, a long counter of thick, unpainted wood, extended for a distance across the back of the noisy, smoke-filled room. No mirror graced the wall behind it, only shelves well stocked with bottles of liquor. There were no glasses to be seen and, watching, Laverty saw one of the three bartenders reach down under the counter to procure one. It came up dripping wet, making it apparent that in lieu of washing, the glasses were merely dipped in a water-filled container of some kind.

Arranged in one section of the saloon were various devices to satisfy those customers with the inclination to gamble: roulette, chuck-a-luck, three-card monte, dice, poker, and any other game a player might fancy. Scattered elsewhere in the room were sturdily built tables and chairs for those who wished to do their drinking sitting down. At the moment all were occupied by soldiers, civilians, and attendant saloon women.

"You looking for company, cowboy?"

At the question Tom turned, faced a short, plump girl dressed in a yellow, low-cut, knee-high dress. She had bangles in her reddish hair, and her features, despite an application of rouge and powder, revealed her weariness.

"No," Tom said, "leastwise not now. Maybe later."

"Later I'll probably be busy, but you can ask—"

The woman paused as a man directly behind her abruptly rose to his feet and lunged across the table at the one facing him. Together they went to the floor amid a clatter of breaking glass and the thud of overturned furniture.

Laverty glanced around. No one other than a third man at the table appeared to notice the sudden conflict. Such was all too common, he supposed—and it explained the crude, strongly built furnishings at King's Castle.

"What's your name if I start asking for you?" Laverty said, raising his voice to be heard above the scuffling and cursing of the two men thrashing about nearby. He could use a bit of feminine company once he got Henry Pettibone's daughter off his mind.

"Nellie—"

Tom nodded. Across the room on the dance floor another fight had broken out, and as before few paused to watch.

"Fine, Nellie. Just may get a chance to look you up. Got somebody else on my mind right now. You happen to know a girl by the name of Louanne Pettibone? Not sure if she works here or not but—"

"The hell with you!" Nellie snapped, abruptly angry. "I don't play second fiddle to nobody!" Wheeling about, she flounced off into the confusion of persons in the room.

"Hold off, wait! I don't mean what you're thinking," Tom called after her. But Nellie either could not or did not wish to hear.

Laverty shrugged. The girl's ire posed no problem; he'd talk to one of the bartenders—which he guessed was what he should have done in the first place. Pulling away from the wall, Tom started to cross the room. He halted. Lieutenant Joseph and a thick-shouldered corporal appeared in the doorway. They paused there momentarily, and then moved on into the noise and drifting smoke saturating the saloon.

Joseph and the non-com headed for the bar, their appearance silencing the uniformed men as well as civilians close by. Reaching the counter, the lieutenant held a brief conversation with one of the bartenders and then hurried off into the crowd with the corporal at his heels. Joseph no doubt was endeavoring to learn the identity of the man who had earlier shot the gambler, which would indicate that he had learned nothing in the saloon called the Paris where the killing was said to have taken place.

Tom watched the young officer and the corporal work their way through the steadily increasing crowd as soldiers and civilians alike continued to enter in singles, pairs, and small groups. Joseph halted now and then to talk with one of the women, and then disappeared finally through one of the two doors in the rear of the building.

Dismissing the two uniformed men from his mind, Laverty stepped into one of the few vacant places at the bar. Placing a foot on the length of thick timber that served as a foot rail, he leaned forward on the heavy plank counter. One of the bartenders came up to him immediately, question on his ruddy features.

"Yeh?"

"Whiskey—and some information."

The barkeep took a dripping glass from the container below, swiped at it with a towel, and then, setting it in front of Tom, filled it from a nearby bottle.

"Whiskey'll be two bits. No charge for the information."

Laverty handed over the required quarter. "I'm looking for a girl—a woman—"

"Lots of them around here, mister."

"Can see that. One I want is named Louanne Pettibone. Was told she might be working here."

The bartender turned away to satisfy the needs of another patron, and shortly returned. "Can't think of nobody by that name. There's one we call Lou here."

"Heard of her—and she could be who I'm looking for. She around now?"

The bartender looked out over the crowd, frowned, and then nodded. "Sure is. That's her, the one wearing the red dress, setting at that table in the corner with them two fellows."

Tom followed the man's pointing finger. He could catch only a half view of the girl and the men she was with as saloon patrons were continually passing back and forth in front of them.

"Think I best give you a bit of advice," the bartender said in a low voice as he bent forward. "If you've got a hankering for her, you best forget it."

Tom frowned. "Why?"

"The jasper she's with, the one all dressed up, is Kurt Morral. On top of that she's sort of special with John King."

The barman stared at Laverty. "Can see now you're a stranger around here. King owns this place and Kurt's one of the Morral brothers—the young one of the three. Morrals have a big ranch east of here in the Cornudo Hills country. Bad medicine, all of them. Other man there is Jess Farley. Friend of Kurt's. Sticks to him like he was his shadow."

"Not looking to marry the girl, just want to talk to her a bit, see if she's who I'm looking for."

"Well, just watch your step. Kurt sort of figures she's his private property."

"Thought you said she sort of belonged to King."

"Reckon she does, but John kind of backs off for the Morrals same as everybody else does."

"Obliged to you for your advice—and I'll sure

watch my step," Laverty said, downing his drink and, drawing away from the counter, started across the floor for the corner table where the girl and the two men were sitting.

8

A HALF-DOZEN steps and Laverty stopped. Lieutenant Joseph and the husky corporal had come out of the room in the rear of the saloon. Following them closely was a tall, well-dressed man. Likely he would be John King, Tom thought.

Laverty remained motionless in the restless crowd as he watched the two uniformed men angle toward the front door, reach it finally, and then disappear into the fading light of day. King also was no longer to be seen but he was somewhere in the saloon, probably over in the area reserved for gambling.

Turning his attention back to the corner where the girl and the two men were sitting, Laverty resumed shouldering his way to them. He was unable to get a clear look at the woman, her back being partly toward him, but the man next to her, undoubtedly Kurt Morral, was about his age, well dressed in a gray flannel shirt, red neckerchief, and a wide-brimmed brown hat that was pushed to the back of his head. Tom could not see the lower part of him very well, it being obscured by the table, but he was wearing new—or newly polished—black boots.

The other man, Jess Farley according to the bartender, was of similar age; he appeared to be a cow-hand, and he sat high on his chair, which would indicate he was tall. Farley had an angular face, wore a black-and-red-checked shirt, scarred boots, and a high-crowned hat that he had removed and placed on the table. Both men glanced up as Laverty halted at their table.

"Keep, moving," Morral said with an imperious jerk of his thumb.

Tom, eyes on the woman, did not move. "Is your name Louanne Pettibone?" he asked.

She had a prettiness that the applications of powder and rouge could not hide. Her hair was dark, as were the thick brows that shaded her blue eyes. A narrow, black ribbon was around her neck and the bright red dress she wore was scooped low to reveal an expanse of arching bosom.

"You hear me?" Morral demanded loudly and angrily. Kurt was drunk and his words were slurred and thick.

"I'm on my way to Cheyenne," Laverty said coolly. "Need to talk to the lady for a couple of minutes. Got something for her if she's who I think she is."

"I don't know you, mister," the woman said in a hard, flat tone. "And whatever you've got for me I'm not interested in."

"It's from your pa—if you're Louanne Pettibone."

The woman frowned. "What makes you think I am?"

"Was told you'd be here in this town," Tom replied,

impatience rising. "Is Pettibone your name or not?"

"You heard what she said! She ain't interested!" Morral shouted. "Now get the hell away from here!"

"Are you Henry Pettibone's daughter?" Laverty said again to the girl.

"You ain't hearing me!" Morral continued loudly. "Told you to move on!"

"Not until I get an answer," Tom said flatly. "I didn't ride all the way up from Arizona to have some drunk put me off. Lady, I want to know if—"

"The hell you do!" Kurt yelled and, coming to his feet, rounded the end of the table.

Eyes burning with anger, mouth distorted, he seized Laverty by the arms. Tom shook loose instantly, spun Morral about, and taking the man by the shoulders, sent him stumbling back into Farley, who had also gotten to his feet.

"Take care of him," Laverty snapped. "My business is with the lady," he added in a barely controlled voice and, turning, faced Lou, who was now standing also. "There some place we can go talk? I've got—"

"Look out!"

At the warning cry from someone in the crowd nearby Laverty whirled, instinct telling him exactly what was happening. Doubling forward, he drew his gun and fired. Morral, his weapon out and leveled, triggered his pistol a fraction of time later, his sagging arm causing the bullet to drive itself harmlessly into the floor.

As smoke boiled up, Tom swerved his attention to

Jess Farley. The tall man, gun half out of his holster, froze. Tom nodded coldly.

"Go ahead. Might as well get this over with."

Farley, indecision claiming him for several breathless moments, relaxed. With a shake of his head he let his weapon settle back into the leather.

Immediately the small crowd that had gathered at the corner came to life. "He's done shot and killed Kurt Morral!" a man leaning over the crumpled figure lying on the dusty floor declared. *"Kurt Morral,* he's killed *him!"*

"Kurt was asking for it—"

"Had his gun out. Just weren't fast enough."

"But Kurt Morral—them brothers of his—friend, I think you sure best make arrangements with the undertaker."

Tom, faint wisps of smoke still hanging about him, tension keeping him tight in its grip, rodded the spent cartridge from his gun and replaced it with a fresh shell from his belt. Gunning a man down was the last thing he had wanted to do, but as he saw it, he had no choice. Holstering the weapon, anger now draining from him, he turned, glanced about for the girl. She was nowhere to be seen.

"What the hell's going on here?"

Tom came back around to face John King. Tall, the dark suit he was wearing riding his lank frame neatly, hair combed flat on his skull, small, close-set eyes like black ice, he stared at Laverty.

"You know what you've done?" King demanded.

"Kept myself from getting a bullet in the back," Tom said evenly. "Your friend there drew first. If somebody in the crowd hadn't sung out, I'd be dead right now."

"Too bad you're not," King said, "but you're just the same as, anyway . . . Somebody go get the marshal."

Activity in the Castle, interrupted by the gunshots, had suspended only briefly and was now once again going full strength. The piano was playing, couples were dancing, and the men at the gambling devices were calling out numbers as if nothing out of the ordinary had happened, and the line at the bar was shoulder to shoulder.

"Who the hell are you?" King asked roughly.

"Name's Tom Laverty. Came up from Arizona looking to—"

"I don't give a goddamn where you came from. All I know is you've brought me more trouble than I want to think about. The Army's raising hell about the shootings in town—had one a bit earlier—and now you've gone and chalked up another one."

King paused, glanced to where Jess Farley and another man were lifting the body of Morral off the floor. "Take him over to Ike's."

"The Morrals will want to bury him on their ranch," Farley said, pausing.

"Know that, but they're not around and I don't want him laying in here."

FARLEY nodded and, with two more volunteers hurrying up to assist, started for the doorway with the limp body.

"You maybe'll get this whole town shut down," King said, eyes bright with anger as he again faced Tom. "Colonel out at the fort's been looking for an excuse. You probably have given it to him."

"Hell, the pilgrim didn't have no choice, Mr. King," a man standing near the saloon owner pointed out. "I was right close and seen it all. You know how Kurt was—he jumped the pilgrim who was only trying to talk to Lou. Then when he pushed Kurt away, Kurt jerked out his gun. He would've plugged the pilgrim right in the back if somebody hadn't hollered."

"You tell that to the colonel and see what it gets you. A killing's a killing as far as he's concerned . . . Where the hell's Fish?"

"Right here," the marshal answered, pushing his way through the circle of men gathered around Tom and the saloon owner. "Seen them carrying Kurt Morral out. Who done it?"

"Man standing right there. Says his name is Tom Laverty. Want you to lock him up till morning, then turn him over to the Army. We'll let the colonel deal with him. Maybe that'll sort of calm him down some."

"The Army won't get no chance if Kurt's brothers show up first," someone noted.

King frowned, pointed a finger at the lawman. "If they do show up, you be damn sure you keep them away from Laverty! He's our only chance to smooth things over with that colonel."

Zack Fish nodded. "Do what I can—but you know that Morral bunch," the marshal said, passing his shotgun to the man beside him to hold. Pistol in his right hand, he reached out to Tom. "Give me your gun, Laverty."

Tom, holding his temper in check, passed the weapon, butt first, to the lawman. "You interested in hearing my side of this? Morral drew first. Plenty of witnesses here who'll tell you that if you'll take time to—"

"Makes no difference," John King cut in. "We've got to satisfy the colonel. Do what I told you, Marshal."

The lawman's jaw hardened and a glint of anger flickered in his pale eyes. For several long moments he did not stir, and then thrusting Laverty's six-gun under his belt, he reclaimed his shotgun, pointed to the doorway, and nodded crisply to Tom.

"Let's go," he said.

9

THE few Castle patrons still interested in the source of the interruption gave way, allowing Laverty and the lawman to pass. Elsewhere in the saloon the gambling, music, dancing, and confusion of other sounds continued unabated.

"You sure as hell tore your britches this time, son," Fish said as they moved out into the street. It was almost full dark and lamps bracketed to the fronts of several buildings along the way cast a yellowish glow over the dusty roadway. "Killing a man is bad enough but you had to go and shoot one of the Morrals! Hell, that's like putting a gun to your own head and pulling the trigger."

The hack and the wagon loaded now with relatively subdued soldiers rumbled by, this time headed for the fort.

"Wasn't my choosing, Marshal. Tried to tell you that, and there's witnesses who'll—"

"What's making things worse," Fish said as if not hearing Laverty at all, "is that right now the damned Army's cracking down on us."

"You're the law. You're supposed to be running things around here," Tom said, seeing an opening that might prove to be in his favor. "How does it happen King and the Army are calling the shots?"

Zack Fish shook his head and muttered something under his breath as they walked on. Despite the recent departure of two dozen or so soldiers, there were still a number of them lolling about along the street as well as those that could be found in the saloons.

"For a fact I am getting a mite tired of being told how to do my job," Fish said after a bit. "Yessir, I sure am."

"Can understand that. Is King sort of the mayor here in Pardo?"

"No, we ain't even got one; it just happens he owns the biggest saloon and gambling house, and the others kind of look to him to be the head man."

Tom shrugged. "Hard to figure how men like the ones in business here would just let somebody take over and run things."

"Hell, they're all too busy making money off the soldiers and pilgrims that come by to pay any attention to who's doing what."

"Zack—"

At the call of his name the lawman laid a hand on Tom's forearm and came to a stop. They were in front of the saloon called the Paris, and as they halted a man came forward to meet them.

"What's the trouble, Nate?" Fish asked. "Some of your girls acting up?" Aside to Laverty he added: "It's Nate Gilmore. Owns the Paris. Always having trouble with his females."

"Heard there was another killing. This the jasper that done it?"

Gilmore was the opposite in appearance to John King. Short, stocky, wearing old baggy pants, a stained white shirt, and heavy shoes, he looked to be a man in from the fields rather than the owner of Pardo's second-largest saloon. He had a broad face covered with a thick mustache and beard, a shock of sand-colored hair on his head, and there was the shine of sweat on his skin despite the coolness of the evening.

"Did you hear that it was in self-defense, too?" Fish asked in a weary voice.

"No, but that don't mean nothing. It won't cut hot butter with that colonel out at the fort. You know what he said: the next one he aimed to—"

"I know what he said," the lawman cut in testily, "and just maybe—"

"Maybe nothing! If we want him to keep from shutting down the whole damn town, or even burning us to the ground like he's been threatening, I figure we best do something about it this time—and do it tonight."

Fish stiffened. "Meaning what?"

"We ought to hold us a trial, find this saddlebum guilty, and string him up. We do that, the Army'll probably be satisfied."

"You talking about a lynching?"

Gilmore shrugged. "Can call it that if you want, but was we to hold a trial tonight—get up a jury and judge and all—it would be a regular legal thing and nobody could fault us for doing it. Zack, we sure got to do something! It'll break me if the Army shuts me down, same as it will a bunch of the others."

The lawman snorted. "You busted! I'll bet you got more cash salted away than most banks! And far as what you're wanting to do being legal, you're wrong. We wouldn't have a real judge running things—and that's what it'd take to make it legal."

Gilmore spat into the dust. "You're splitting hairs. I can't see as it'll be any different. We could make old Ben Levi the judge; he claims to be a lawyer, and we're right careful, choose a jury . . ."

Tom, listening in silence, felt his nerves tighten. Pardo was a wild, ungoverned town and he didn't know how far Zack Fish would go to protect him from a lynch party, disguised as a court of law.

"You been talking to anybody else about this?" the marshal asked after giving Gilmore's words thought.

"Nope, sure haven't; not yet. But I reckon they'd throw right in with the idea. Know Redfern and Parley Kercher would, same with Pete Willoughby over at the saddle shop. Goes for Bert Cassidy, too. Don't think we'd have any trouble lining up the rest of the town 'cepting maybe John King. He's always been so all-fired set on kissing the Army's hind end. Expect he'd want to leave it to that colonel to take care of the killer. I figure the town'll want to do it itself. It'll look better to the Army—"

"I don't give a damn what the Army and John King want or don't want," Fish said, his voice firm. "About time folks, and the Army, realize I'm the marshal of this town and I intend to uphold the law the way I'm supposed!"

Surprise filled Nate Gilmore's eyes. He brushed at his beard as he stared at Fish. "You meaning that?"

"Wouldn't've said it if I didn't."

Gilmore wagged his head. "You're a fool, Zack. You know how long the marshal ahead of you lasted when he started getting high and mighty like you're doing?"

"Don't know, and I sure don't give a hoot. All I know is I was hired to do a job and it just come to me that I best wake up and do it."

"Hell, use your head, Zack! That saddlebum'll end up dead anyway. Expect King told you to hold him for the

Army. What's the difference in us stringing him up tonight and the Army shooting him tomorrow? And if we do it, it'll put us back in that Colonel's good graces."

"You're talking about hanging a man who maybe don't have it coming to him," Zack said impatiently. "He was only protecting himself when he cut down Kurt Morral."

"Maybe so, but that won't count for nothing where the Army—or the other Morrals—are concerned. You're forgetting them, Zack. Ben and Charlie ain't going to let this pass just because King wants the Army to take care of the saddlebum. They'll come pounding in here in the morning after him soon as they've been told what happened, and they'll tear down that jail of yours to get him—and the town won't get no credit at all for doing what it ought."

Three cowhands reeled by, their spurs jingling musically as they staggered from side to side. All were on the verge of collapsing into the dust from the amount of liquor each had consumed, and no doubt would have except for the support they were giving one another.

"Was this the kind of a town I'm used to marshaling," Fish said sourly, "I'd throw them three so far back in the jug it'd take a week to find them!"

"Their kind, and the soldiers, is what keeps this town going," Gilmore said patiently. "This ain't no regular town, Zack, you knew that when you hired on. Place is here to furnish liquor, women, and gambling for any that are looking for it. Don't go trying to change that! Won't be a healthy thing to do."

"Expect you're right," Fish said, anger in his voice, "and it won't be healthy for anybody that tries taking this man away from me. Goes for the town and the Army—and Ben and Charlie Morral!"

Again Nate Gilmore shook his head. "You're dead wrong looking at it the way you are, Zack. And you're making a hell of a mistake. You think you can hold us all off?"

"Can sure try," Fish said, and giving Tom a slight push, resumed the walk to the jail.

The hack and the wagon broke into sight at the far end of the street and shortly rattled by. Both were empty. There would be no more official leave from the fort for the men stationed there, apparently, but those who dared slip out when the backs of sentries were turned could make the few-mile hike to the town and all its irresistible attractions on foot if they so desired.

"You figure to stand off any bunch from town or the Morrals if they come after me?" Tom asked as they neared the jail, a small frame building standing off to one side along the street. A lot of yelling was going on over at the depot where a number of soldiers were climbing aboard for another return trip to the fort.

"Was talking mostly," Fish said, turning to watch the activity at the depot. "Was wanting to cool Gilmore down a mite. If he gets up a pretty fair mob, I won't have a chance of holding them off."

"Can give me back my gun. Can sure put up a fight then."

"Yeh, I reckon we could, but it would mean a lot of killings, and that would give that colonel all the more reason to wipe out the town—not that it'd matter anything to me because I'd likely be dead.

"Point is I've been a lawman all my life, and I know the idea of hanging a man who don't deserve stringing up is not only wrong but it's something I plain can't swallow. Never was guilty of letting it happen, and I don't feel like starting in now."

"Not likely that you can stop them," Tom said as they entered the dimly lit jail. "But I sure am obliged to you for wanting to try."

"Well, it ain't done yet," Zack said, turning up the lamp and ushering Torn into one of the cells. Locking the grille door, he added: "I've got a powerful lot of thinking to do. Could be I'll come up with a good idea."

10

TOM crossed the small cage and dropped onto the slat cot that occupied one side. There were two other cells, he noted, neither of which was occupied. It was one hell of a note, he thought: here he was behind iron bars, in a town that believed in lynch law, and all he had set out to do was a favor for a good friend. Instead of accomplishing that it was likely he'd end up swinging from a rope.

Tom glanced up, looked into the adjoining room where Zack Fish maintained his office. The lawman was seated at the table that served as a desk, leafing through a stack of papers, probably wanted dodgers on outlaws. It was to be expected, but Zack was wasting his time; he'd never been guilty of anything more serious than a few Saturday night saloon brawls, Tom knew.

The clattering of the wagon followed by that of the hack came from the street as the conveyances again made a return trip from the fort. Somewhere down in front of the saloon row someone was singing in a loud, cracked voice. Elsewhere along the way there was laughter and yelling. A soldier appeared in the doorway of the jail, red face wreathed in smiles, hair awry and uniform blouse unbuttoned and dusty.

"Howdy, Sheriff! How's it going?" he asked in a thick voice, and moved on.

"Don't those men have to report back to the fort at night?" Tom asked.

"Sure, unless they've got leave," the lawman replied. "And them that don't can sneak out and come back, if they want."

"Sounds like things are mighty loose out there."

"Yeh, reckon it seems that way. But there ain't much going on to keep the men busy—like fighting Indians and such—so the colonel just sort of lets them do what they want long as they don't get out of hand."

"I thought he was all fired up to close down the town."

"The killings are what makes him look at it that way. That jasper that shot the gambler, and you killing

Morral—them and the ones before are what's riled him up so. Like as not in another hour or two you'll see a squad ride in here and round up every uniform in town and head them back to the fort."

"Sort of get things ready for in the morning when the colonel comes after me, that it?"

"If the Morrals or a town lynch mob don't get to you first," Fish said laconically. "I've been doing some thinking about that."

"What about my right for a fair trial?" Laverty said, rising and moving to the front of his cell. "Ain't I due that?"

The lone songbird had progressed along the street until he was now opposite the jail. When his quavery, discordant voice began to fill the small building with raucous sound, Fish abruptly forsook his chair and stepped to the doorway.

"Cut out that damn howling unless you want me to throw you in the jug!" the lawman shouted irritably, and as the singing ended suddenly, came back around and resumed his chair. "Sure you've got the right," he said, "but around here that don't mean much. It's what the bunch that runs things here, and the Army, want. And in your case I expect we better say the Morrals, too."

"You could sneak me out sometime tonight, take me to another town where I'd get a fair shake."

"Been thinking what to do, and maybe—" Fish began, and broke off. "Why, howdy, Lou. What can I do for you?"

Tom edged to the end of his cell where he had a better view of the doorway. It was the woman he had been trying to talk to when Kurt Morral turned the conversation into a shoot-out.

"I'd like to talk to your prisoner, Marshal, if it's all right."

Fish got to his feet. "Can't see no harm in that," he said, taking the ring of keys off a nail in the wall behind him and leading the way to the cells.

"Lady wants to talk to you," he said as Tom backed up to the cot. Unlocking the grille, he let the woman enter and then closed and relocked the door. "When you want out, Lou, just holler."

The girl, standing just within the cage, remained silent for several moments and then moved slowly over to the cot where Laverty was still standing.

"Mite surprised to see you," Tom said. "Have a seat," and as she settled on the slatted arrangement, took a place beside her.

Lou had thrown a knitted shawl over her shoulders but he could see she still had on the bright red dress she was wearing in the saloon. The only change was that she had washed the rouge and powder from her face, which gave her a younger, fresher look.

"Expect you want me to say I'm sorry for what happened back there in the Castle," she said in a firm, remorseless voice, "but you know what Kurt's like. Always ready to—"

"No, I didn't know what he was like," Tom cut in, anger aroused by the woman's lack of regret. "I'd

74

never seen him before today."

Lou frowned. "Then you are a stranger around here?"

Tom nodded. "I am . . . Are you Louanne Pettibone?"

"Yes, that's my real name. I'm called Lou Petty around here. You said you had something for me, or to tell me?"

Laverty studied the woman closely. She could be Henry Pettibone's daughter—or she just might say she was and hope to gain something by doing so.

"Maybe. Mind telling me what your ma's name was?"

Lou's eyes hardened with anger. "You doubting my word?" she demanded, and then as if realizing what Laverty had said, added, "Did you say *was?* That mean she's dead?"

"Afraid so."

"Well, I'm her daughter. Her name was Anne and Pa's name was Henry Louis. They called me Louanne after themselves."

"I reckon you're who I'm looking for," Laverty said, reaching inside his shirt for the pouch Pettibone had entrusted to him. "Your pa and me were good friends," he added as he handed her the leather sack. "He's dead, too."

A sigh escaped Lou's lips. She was pretty, Tom realized as he studied her there in the glow of the lamp with her hair glinting softly and her face, devoid of all cosmetics, looking clean and fresh.

"Both of them dead," she murmured. Her attitude changed from guarded and almost belligerent to one more conciliatory. "I had hoped to go back home someday and see them, but somehow I never got around to it."

"You ma died soon after you left. Your pa was killed about a month ago."

Lou looked up, a frown on her face. "How?"

"It wasn't something bad," Laverty said, realizing what she was thinking. "We were popping steers out of the brush on a ranch down on the San Pedro River—that's in Arizona—when an old mossy horn gored him."

"Then he was hurt, not shot or anything like that. Couldn't something be done for him?"

"Happened quite a piece from the ranch. Time the wagon got there to haul him back it was too late."

"Arizona?" Lou said, as if again suddenly realizing what Tom had said. "Our home was in Tennessee, and Papa was a preacher, not a cowboy."

"I guess things just sort of fell apart after you ran off. And then when your ma died, Henry, your pa, gave up preaching and started drifting around the country. I met him when he signed on to work for Jeremiah Madden."

"Hard for me to think of him being a cowboy—"

"Was a real greenhorn all right, but he caught on fast and he never backed away from anything. He was my partner."

Lou opened the pouch and shook its contents out

into her lap: four double eagles and the cameo. She took up the gold chain from which the locket was suspended and slowly examined it. Oval in shape, it was of gold filigree, and the carved full-length figure of a woman, hair and dress streaming in the wind, was a delicate gray and stood out in sharp relief from the stone. Releasing the catch, Lou opened the bit of jewelry.

"Their pictures," she murmured, and holding the locket open for Laverty to see, exhibited daguerreotype likenesses of her parents in the small spaces provided for each.

"Your ma was a real pretty woman," Tom said.

"Yes, she was. Did Papa still look like his picture?" she asked, closing the locket.

"Could say he did . . . He was real sorry that he didn't have more to give you."

"The cameo is all that really counts. It's very valuable, Mama once told me. It belonged to her grandmother, was passed down to her. She was to give it to me and I was to pass it on to my daughter, when I had one—which doesn't seem likely."

"Why not? You're young and certainly a—"

"Do you think that counts for much, me being what I am today—a saloon woman?"

"You could leave here, start a new life where nobody knows you. That money your pa left you will take you a far piece."

"Yes, I guess it would. I really haven't been anyplace. When I left home, I wound up in St. Louis. Met a man there, a cattle buyer who took me to Dodge City. Was there for a time with him, then I came here, on my own. Heard there was a lot of money to be made in Pardo. The rumor was only partly right. Soldiers spend money like there was no tomorrow, all right, but they just don't ever make much."

"Saw quite a few cowhands hanging around the saloons—"

"Sure, but they're pretty much in the same boat. Hardly ever have any cash unless they get lucky gambling—which isn't often. Did I hear you say you were going to Cheyenne? That's up in Wyoming, isn't it?"

"What I was planning to do. Getting locked up sort of changes things. They're holding me for murder."

"I know. I heard King talking about it to some of the other merchants. They plan to turn you over to the colonel at the fort, and hope it will satisfy him. He's all worked up over the killings that have gone on here in Pardo. Some of the men shot were soldiers."

Lou put the gold eagles back into the pouch and placed it in the reticule she was carrying.

"It's not right what they're doing to you!" she said suddenly. "They're making you the goat."

"Maybe the colonel won't get the chance to stand me up before a firing squad if the Morral brothers get here first—or some of the others in town who don't agree with King and take it into their heads to string me up."

Laverty shrugged, hesitated as he listened to some unintelligible shouting coming from nearby in the street. "Things sure work out funny sometimes."

Lou brushed at some imagined dust in her lap. "And all because you wanted to do me—and Papa—a favor." Abruptly the woman got to her feet and crossed to the front of the cell. "Marshal!" she called.

Zack Fish, standing in the doorway, attention on something taking place up the street, turned.

"Yeh?"

"Want to tell you something."

The lawman doubled back to the cells. "If it's about Laverty, I expect I know already what you're going to say."

"He shouldn't be in here," Lou stated flatly, ignoring the lawman's words. "I was right there when it started; in fact it was sort of over me. Mr. Laverty here only wanted to talk to me, but Kurt, well, you know how he was. Thought he owned me.

"Mr. Laverty was walking away when Kurt drew his gun. Somebody yelled a warning and Mr. Laverty—"

"Tom," Laverty corrected.

"And Tom turned in time to shoot Kurt before Kurt could shoot him. If he hadn't, he wouldn't be here now."

"Know all that," Fish said. "He's not guilty of murder."

"Then why can't you just let him go? You're the law here. Seems you'd have the right to."

"Been thinking all that over," the marshal said. "But you've got to remember I work for the town, for John King and all the rest of the saloon keepers and merchants and—"

"You're still the law. How can they make you do something you know is wrong?" Lou said as she hung the cameo about her neck.

Fish wheeled abruptly and walked quickly to the doorway. Again he turned his attention up the street in the direction of the saloons. He remained there for only a moment and then hurriedly retraced his steps to the cells.

"Want you to get out of here fast, Lou," he said, unlocking the cage.

"Why—what—"

"Don't go asking questions. Trouble's coming. Now, go around the back way so you won't be seen."

The woman stepped out of the cell. Fish slammed the door shut and turned the lock.

"I want to thank you, Tom," Lou said, "and tell you that I'm sorry I got you into this. Good luck!"

"We'll both be needing plenty of that," Fish snapped. "Now, get out of here!"

11

TOM watched the girl cross to the exit and step out into the cool, half-bright night. Zack Fish followed her to the opening, halting just inside to throw his glance up the street once more. Immediately he turned back to Laverty.

"I'm deputizing you," the lawman said in a hurried voice.

"Me, a deputy?" Tom said. "I'm your prisoner. How can you make me a deputy?"

"There's a lynch mob coming down the street led by Nate Gilmore. They aim to string you up. Listen close. Do you swear by God to uphold the laws of the territory of New Mexico?"

"Sure, but I don't savvy how you can—"

"That makes you my lawful deputy," Fish said, and handed Tom the ring of keys. "Here's how we're doing this. You stay locked in that cell unless I yell for you. If I do, it'll mean I can't stop that bunch and need your help—and quit worrying about me deputizing a prisoner. You won't be one any longer if this works out."

Tom grinned, nodded. "Obliged to you, Marshal. My gun, I best have it."

"It'll be laying there on my desk. You can pick it up when you come out—if I holler for you." The lawman paused, gave Tom a searching look. "I'm depending on you not to cross me up and make a run for it."

"I won't," Laverty said, and glanced to the door. The sound of voices in the street could be heard along with the scuffing and thudding of heavy shoes and boots on the sunbaked ground.

"I reckon they're here," Fish said, and crossed to the table that served as his desk. Opening the drawer, he removed Laverty's .45 and laid it on the top. Then taking up his shotgun, the marshal stepped out onto the small landing that fronted the building. Tom watched him raise the double-barrel, a squat, resolute figure in the half dark, and level it at the approaching mob.

"All of you—hold up right where you are!"

The sound of voices and scrape of boots and shoes ceased.

"Back off, Zack!" It was Gilmore. He was evidently the leader of the mob, as the lawman had suspected he would be. "You won't be no part of this unless you make it so."

"I'm the marshal here and it's my duty to make it so," Fish snapped. "You're not taking my prisoner, make up your minds to that. Now move on, go about your business."

"This here is our business!" someone yelled. "Hanging that drifter for killing Kurt Morral is the only way we'll get the Army off our backs."

"You're fooling yourself, Parley. Lynching the man won't help a bit. Anyway King and the colonel's idea is to put him on trial."

"We do it our way, the colonel won't have to bother putting him on trial—and I'm laying odds that'll suit him a lot better. Now, get out of our way, Zack. We're going to do what we started out—"

"No!" Fish cut in sharply.

Triggering the shotgun, he sent a charge of buckshot into the direction of Nate Gilmore and the men backing him. The pellets apparently plowed into the ground somewhere in front of the saloon keeper and the mob, stopping them short as the smell of dust and gunpowder suddenly filled the air.

"Hell, that old scattergun ain't going to hold us back," someone shouted after the echoes had died. "You only got one more barrel—and you never was much with a six-gun."

"Maybe not," Zack said evenly, "but my deputy sure is."

"Deputy?" Gilmore echoed.

"Just what I said," Fish replied as he reloaded the shotgun, and without turning, shouted: "Come on out, Deputy!"

Tom opened the cell immediately and, crossing the room to the lawman's desk, snatched up his gun. Checking the cylinder to be certain it was still fully loaded, he slid it into the holster and stepped out into the street.

"Him!" Nate Gilmore said in a disbelieving voice. "You made that killer your deputy?"

"Why not? There weren't no reason for him being locked up in the first place."

"The hell there wasn't! He shot and killed Kurt Morral!"

"Kurt made the first move. There's a plenty of witnesses to that."

There were no soldiers on the street, Tom noticed, but there were several standing in the doorway of the Paris. Evidently they had slipped away from the fort and didn't want to become involved in an incident that would prove they had been AWOL.

"Now, maybe I ain't no great shakes with a six-gun, but I reckon you know my deputy is," Fish said coolly.

"Telling you again to move on."

"Making him a deputy ain't legal!" a voice declared. "It can't be."

"It's legal," the marshal said in the same confident tone. "I swore him in just like I did you and the others, Abe, the time we had to track down that woman killer. It's my right to do that when I'm needing help to uphold the law."

There was a muttering of uncertainty among the men. Finally someone said: "Oh hell, let's just forget it."

"Yeh, let the colonel handle it," another added.

"Or the Morrals . . . You think you can hold Ben and Charlie off when they show up, Zack?"

"Aim to try," the lawman said. "Now, are you moving on or you want some of this buckshot in your legs?"

There was another lengthy silence while the haunting strains of "Auralee" sung in a high soprano voice drifted along the street from one of the saloons. Abruptly the mob began to break up, the men to stir about uncertainly, and then in pairs and small groups head back toward the business district. Shortly only Nate Gilmore and two other men remained. They continued to stare at Zack and Tom Laverty for a long minute and then they too turned about and shuffled off into the shadowy roadway.

"How long'll it take you to get out of town?" Fish said when they were again alone.

"Only have to get my horses from the livery stable,"

Tom replied as they entered the jail.

"Best I do that; don't want somebody seeing you. I'll go get them and—"

The sudden hammer of hooves brought Fish around. Looking up the street, he swore deeply.

"It's the Morrals. Got to get you out of sight."

LOU PETTY threw a quick look over her shoulder as Zack Fish hurried her out the door. A crowd of a dozen or so men was advancing on the jail. One was waving a rope above his head as he yelled at a bystander along the way. Lou's throat tightened. Lynch mob! And they were coming for Tom Laverty!

"Can't I do something? Can't I go get help?" she asked anxiously, turning to Fish.

The lawman shook his head. "There ain't nobody in this town that'd turn a hand at a time like this. Most folks around here dote on killings—and lynchings. Just you get away from here. Me and Tom can take care of ourselves."

Lou hesitated briefly and then, hurrying on, circled the building. As she drew abreast the high window in the rear wall of the jail, Laverty's voice, strong and clear, came to her.

"Me, a deputy? I'm a prisoner, how can I be a deputy?"

Zack's reply was barely audible but it had to do with Gilmore and the lynch mob in the street. The marshal was planning to face them down, and he would call on Tom to come to his aid if it became necessary. And when it was all over, and they were still alive, Laverty would be free to go. Zack Fish had apparently decided there was no cause to keep Tom locked up any longer.

Lou sighed in relief. Tom Laverty should be allowed to go. He had done only what any man would do: protect himself. She had hoped all along that he would be released, and wanted to believe that what she had said to the marshal had something to do with his being freed. But whether it had or not, Tom would be out of it as soon as the lynch mob was turned back, and she had little doubt now that Tom would be backing the marshal.

She liked the big six-foot cowhand with the calm gray eyes, and wished that she might have become better acquainted with him. He had gone to a great deal of trouble to fulfill the promise he had made to her father.

Lou wondered idly if it were possible to do as he had suggested: leave, break away from Pardo and the past, and start a new life somewhere. It didn't sound too difficult the way he had said it, and thinking about it, she reckoned it wouldn't be if she made up her mind to it.

There was no longer the sound of voices coming from the jail and she guessed that Tom and the marshal were out in the street confronting the lynch mob. Strangely, she had no fear that they could accomplish what they planned to do. Tom Laverty knew how to use a six-gun, that was certain, and most likely many of the men in the mob had witnessed his ability. Zack

Fish should have no trouble breaking up the mob now and sending the men on their way.

Could she start over? Could she go somewhere and build a new life for herself, the kind that her father no doubt had believed she was leading? She had a little money put back, and with the gold eagles he had sent her, she'd have a stake, a small one to be sure, but enough to permit her leaving Pardo and John King and his Castle, and the life of a saloon woman who earned a small living by satisfying the lust of soldiers and other men.

She had a horse and a gun. They had been given her by a man who came west to be a cowboy but found the life not what he had thought it would be and, disillusioned, had returned to his family home in the east.

Lou had little use for the animal, a small sorrel mare, and had ridden it only a few times. Not that she didn't enjoy a sashay out across the gray hills and flats; it was simply that she seldom ever had the opportunity. It had been her intention to sell the horse, but buyers were few and she had let the matter rock along, stabling the mare in a small shed near the one-room shack where she lived.

Voices in the street had grown louder and she guessed the confrontation was getting hot. Suddenly a gunshot sounded and, pausing as she moved slowly away from the rear of the jail, she tried to hear what was being said. There was considerable talking and then Zack Fish's raised voice came to her.

"Come on out, Deputy!"

There was a lot more conversation after that, and Lou, keeping to the shadows, made her way forward along the side of the jail until she could look into the street.

The lawman, now sided by Tom Laverty, had halted the mob. There was considerable quibbling going on, protests, arguments, and threats, but no one was making any move toward Laverty and the marshal. And no one would. Lou knew most of the men in the crowd; they talked big but there was never anything behind their words. Sooner or later they would back off and head for one of the saloons where they'd nurture their wavering courage with a few drinks.

In the hush that suddenly lay over the crowd, the song "Auralee" reached her. Lou recognized the voice of Stella, one of the women who also worked for King. A faded, worn-out blonde, she had been with King since he opened the Castle and likely, as Lou had heard her say often, would die there.

That recollection abruptly brought Lou to a decision. She would leave! She'd seize the opportunity that very night, gathering up what few belongings meant anything, saddle her horse, and head north. In doing so immediately, she'd be a long way from Pardo before John King discovered she was gone. Throwing a glance at the crowd, she turned her back to the street and hurried off into the darkness for her shack.

12

T OM crossed to the door, looked toward the saloon where two riders had stopped. Both were dismounting and moving up to the hitch rack.

"The one wearing that old Rebel army hat's Ben," Fish said at Laverty's shoulder. "Other one's his brother, Charlie."

In the poor light and the distance separating King's Castle from the jail, Tom could not tell much about the Morrals. Ben was a squat, thick-shouldered man with little if any neck, and a tough, swaggering way about him. His tall bay horse appeared even from where he stood, head down, to have been ridden hard.

Charlie Morral, a large, burly man, sported a high-crowned Texas hat. In lieu of a shirt he wore the top half of his underwear, which contrasted starkly with the black leather vest he had pulled on. Both had knee-high brush boots with the legs of their dark-colored pants tucked inside.

"They'll be coming here," the marshal said, "but I reckon it won't be for a spell. First off they'll have to swallow down a few drinks in King's place while they do their talking and finding out what happened and who shot Kurt, then they'll be going down to Ike Bellwood's to see about the body. After that we can expect them to come here looking for you."

"Thought somebody said their ranch was quite a

ways from here. Sure didn't take them long to show up."

"They must've been somewhere close—and some jasper wanting to show them he's a friend probably busted a gut getting the word to them . . . We've got maybe an hour to get you out of town."

Laverty considered that for a few moments as he leaned against the wall of the marshal's office. "How's this all going to work out for you? Seems to me the Morrals'll blame you for letting me go, and take it all—"

"Don't worry none about that. If they try—"

"Hell, Marshal," Laverty cut in, "I'm not riding out of here and leaving you to face them alone."

"And don't fret about that either. Something like this has been coming for a long time. Made up my mind I'm done bowing and scraping to the likes of them. I'm the law and I figure it's time I raised up on my hind legs and let everybody know it."

"From what I've heard they're a pair of real bad hard cases. Don't think you'll stand much chance bucking them alone."

"Well, now, I ain't so sure they're all that tough! All they've ever done around here is push folks around. I don't think Charlie or Ben ever faced up to an even-steven gunfight; neither did Kurt."

"But you can't bet on that."

Fish grinned wryly, pulled off his narrow-brimmed hat, and rubbed at his balding pate. "No, reckon not, but I expect I can scrape up a couple of friends—Ike

Bellwood for one—if I have to . . . Now here's what I'm fixing to do. Said you'd left your horses at the livery stable; that'd be Ike's."

Tom nodded. "Only barn I saw."

"There's a couple back off the street but Ike's the one most everybody uses. You go set yourself down on that cot in your cell. Ain't no need to lock the door unless the Morrals show up, which I'm pretty sure they won't; not for a while, anyways. Jaspers like them have got to sort of fortify themselves with liquor before they do anything.

"And Gilmore and his bunch ain't likely to be back. We took all the starch out of them out there in the street."

"You don't figure I could slip out around the back and get to Bellwood's without anybody seeing me?"

"Doubt it. There's always somebody wandering around the street and the buildings, and being right famous all of a sudden like you are, you'd be spotted for sure."

Laverty said nothing for a long breath, then: "Why don't I just stay put and have it out with these Morrals? Expect I can hold my own with them."

"Yeh, maybe you could, but what about the Army? What about Nate Gilmore? You figure you can take them on, too, and still end up among the living? No, best we do this my way. Where you aiming to go?"

"Cheyenne. Been wanting to see it—and the Wyoming country."

"Cheyenne, eh. Well, when you leave here, get over

to the river and head north. You'll come to the Crossing, about twenty-five miles from here. Next place'll be Rayado, a sort of a settlement. About fifteen or sixteen miles farther on—"

"How far to the Colorado line?" Tom broke in.

"Ain't such a far piece. Cimarron town is about twelve miles on past Rayado. I expect it's some forty miles on to Colorado from there, and if you can make that without any trouble, you'll be doing fine.

"There's a town called Trinidad just across the border, a little ways. Lawman there's named Henline. He's hard-nosed and tough, but straight as a ridgepole. If you've got anybody trailing you, go to him. Tell him I said for you to look him up and say howdy for me, and that I'll be obliged to him for any favors he can do for you."

"You're figuring the Army'll be looking for me?"

"Not them so much, or Gilmore and his bunch either. Once you're long gone from here, they'll probably back off. It's the Morrals you'll have to worry about. They ain't the forgetting kind. Now, I'll keep them hanging around here long as I can so's you can get a good start."

Tom shook his head in dissatisfaction. Out in the street more singing and loud talking could be heard. Additional soldiers had apparently slipped away from the fort and were enjoying themselves in the town. A strange, wayward thought came to Laverty: was Louanne Pettibone—or Lou Petty as she now called herself—among the revelers? It seemed a shame that

Henry's daughter, so young and pretty, and in whom he set such store, was leading that kind of life. But that was her business and he had no right to interfere.

"Still don't feel right pulling out and leaving you to face all this trouble alone."

"It ain't worrying me none. I've been in worse tights over Kansas way when I was sheriffing, and there's always the chance some of the merchants here in town will find a little backbone somewhere and stand up for me. The Morrals ain't all that popular around here."

Tom shrugged and moved slowly into his cell. Closing the door, he sat down on the cot. Fish halted just outside the bars.

"Here's the key," he said, handing the ring to Tom. "If you hear somebody trying to bust in, you do what you think best: either lock the cell or figure to use your gun. I'd say locking yourself up will be the smart thing but I don't think you'll be having any trouble. Just set quiet till I get back. I'll be locking the outside door anyway," Fish added as he turned and started across the room. "Anybody comes along and wants to get in will find it won't be easy."

"Whatever you say, Marshal," Tom, said resignedly. "Still would as soon take my chances going after my horses and riding out, but I expect you know best. How long do you figure it'll take you?"

"Aim to scout around a bit, see for sure where the Morrals are. Want to know exactly where we stand, then I'll go get your horses. I'd guess I'll be gone about thirty minutes."

Laverty swore softly. "Going to be a long half hour."

"I'll do my best to make it sooner. Now, when you hear something going on out behind the jail, don't get jumpy. That'll be me. There's a shed out there I'll put your horses in, then I'll come around, open the door so's you can slip out and get to them."

"I'll be right here waiting," Laverty said dryly. "If—"

The sound of horses approaching the jail cut into Tom's words. The marshal glanced out into the street. He muttered a curse and wheeled to Tom.

"Lock that cell door—and keep that gun hid!" he said in a quick, tense voice. "It's—"

"Evening, Marshal," a voice from the outside reached Laverty.

"Why, howdy, Lieutenant, what's on your mind?" the lawman responded.

"The colonel sent me in with a couple of men. Give me orders to post a guard over your prisoner . . . Dismount!"

The creaking of leather followed the young officer's command. "Expect he wants to be sure the killer'll be here in the morning—alive."

LOU PETTY stuffed the last of the clothing she wanted and certain other possessions into the flour sack and cinched the opening closed with a piece of cord.

"You can have my dresses and anything else I've left behind," she said to Zarah, who was her closest friend in a town where close friends were scarce. "I don't want to ever see them again!"

Zarah, small, dark, and with a trace of Mexican blood in her veins, gathered up the pile of red, blue, and yellow garments.

"Of this you are sure?"

"Dead sure. I'll never work in a saloon again even if it means starving! I'm quitting this kind of life for good."

Zarah studied Lou with doubtful, dark eyes. "What else can you do? Like me you have never done anything but work in a saloon."

Lou drew on her wool jacket. She had changed clothing, now was dressed in a man's pair of pants previously cut down to fit, a dark, linsey-woolsey shirt, and high-button shoes. She had wrapped a red scarf about her head and was now placing upon it a narrow-brimmed hat.

"I'll find something," she said. "I was working in a dressmaker's shop for a short time in Dodge, enough to say I've had some experience. That was before I met John King. Expect I can find decent work of some kind."

"You have money enough to last till you do?" Zarah asked. "I have a little that you—"

"Thank you," Lou said, reaching out and touching the woman on the arm, "but I've got the money that Papa sent me, and about thirty dollars that I've been able to save."

Lou paused, glanced about. They were in one of the small, crude shacks standing at the rear of the Castle that served as quarters for the women working for King.

"I guess that's everything," she murmured. "I've got my horse ready, a lunch packed, so I guess the next thing to do is leave."

Zarah came to her feet at once and, dropping the dresses into the chair she'd been sitting in, threw her arms about Lou. "I hope you know what you are doing, *querida*."

"I do," Lou said firmly. "Getting that money from Papa, and hearing what that cowhand, Tom Laverty, had to say gave me the push to do what I should have done a long time ago . . . I'll miss you, Zarah."

"And I'll miss you. Do you have the gun?"

Lou nodded, patted the pocket of her jacket. "It's the revolver that boy from New York gave me. I've only shot it a couple of times, but I expect I can use it if I run into trouble." Taking up the flour sack of her belongings and another that contained food for the trail, Lou started for the door. "I guess this is good-bye."

Zarah hurried to open the door. "I guess it is. Do you still not want to tell me where you are going—in case—"

"No, it's best you don't know. King won't be able to beat it out of you then."

"I'd never tell him anyway, but it is wise to be careful. That cowboy you told me about, the one who shot Kurt—what of him?"

"He has probably gone by now; the marshal was

going to turn him loose. There's not much chance of his coming to find me, but if he does, tell him I did what he wanted me to do—and that I'm much obliged to him."

"I will tell him," Zarah said, and glanced toward the Castle. "Someone comes. It is best you go."

Lou was already moving toward the dark shadows where she had left her horse.

"Good luck," Zarah called softly into the night.

"Same to you," Lou replied in a low voice.

13

A IN'T that a mite unusual, Lieutenant?" Zack Fish said in a mildly protesting voice. "This here man's a civilian prisoner."

"Maybe. The colonel doesn't aim to interfere, Marshal. The killing took place right here in town so it's up to the town to punish him; leastways that's how the colonel looks at it. He just wants to be certain that everything goes off without a hitch. Your Mr. King agrees with what we're doing."

"He ain't my Mr. King!" Fish snapped. "But I reckon you've got your orders and that's how it'll be."

"Then it's all right with you if I post these two men inside the jail?"

Zack Fish slid a sidelong look at Laverty. Tom was in the cell lounging on the cot. He had closed the barred door, but there had been no time to lock it.

"Reckon I ain't got a choice," the lawman said.

Lieutenant Joseph half turned, motioned to the two uniformed men waiting in the half dark outside the building. "Davis, you and Morgan get inside, find a place to sit where you won't be seen."

"Yes, sir, Lieutenant," Davis, the older of the pair, said, and stepped up to the doorway. He paused there until Morgan joined him. "Anything else, sir?"

"No, stay here until you're relieved in the morning," Joseph replied, responding to the salutes of the two enlisted men. Then, coming about, he nodded to Zack Fish, stepped out into the street, and mounting his horse, rode off. Moments later Davis and Morgan entered the lawman's office and settled onto one of the benches placed against the wall.

The marshal remained in the doorway for several moments as if in deep thought. Finally he turned, crossed to Laverty's cell. There was a tight smile on his weathered face.

"Sure didn't figure on this," he murmured.

"Know that," Tom said in a low voice, "but don't get all upset about it. Just get my horses. It'll work out."

"This the bird that sent Kurt Morral to the bone-yard?"

Tom hushed instantly at the soldier's words. Fish half turned, nodded. "Yep, sure is."

"We heard he had a good reason," one of them said.

Davis, the corporal, nodded. "Far as I'm concerned any reason was good enough to plug Morral. He was a bad one, and if any man ever had a bullet coming to him, it was him. What's the prisoner's name?"

"Tom Laverty," Fish said.

"What do you reckon they'll do to him?"

"Hang him; that's what the lieutenant said the town was supposed to do, and what the colonel's expecting. Heard the sarge say this morning that he wants the town to make an example of this dude," Davis said.

"Even if he don't have it coming? Kind of a raw deal if you ask me."

"Well, nobody is—and anyway the Army ain't famous for giving a man a fair shake if it suits their purpose not to . . . Marshal, you got some drinking water around here?"

"Bucket and dipper there back of my desk," Fish replied, pointing.

"I'm mighty sore and dry, too," Morgan said, following the corporal back into the adjoining room. "Sarge had me riding that damn blue this morning. By God, I ain't never seen such a stinking, ridge-backed, hard-mouthed bag of bones in my whole life!"

"Cheer up, Morg," Davis said unfeelingly as he filled the dipper. "You wanted to be in the cavalry; and anyway the colonel says we got to use every piece of equipment."

"Well, I wish to hell he was the one making use of that blue! Ain't never seen a meaner, contrarier critter in my whole life," Morgan said, dipping himself a drink from the bucket. "You bring your cards?"

Davis shook his head as he sat down on one of the benches. "Nope, sure didn't. The lieutenant didn't give me time to do nothing."

Morgan cursed, and sank down beside his partner. "Sure going to be a long night," he said mournfully.

Fish and Tom Laverty had listened in silence to the soldiers, and, when both had finally settled, the lawman moved up closer to the bars of the cell.

"Don't know what you're thinking but anything'll beat being here in the morning," he said quietly.

Tom nodded grimly. "Way they've got it worked out I won't have a chance."

"Sure about the size of it. What do you want me to do?"

Laverty was silent for a few moments. Then, "Best you don't get mixed up in what happens next. Just get my horses and I'll take care of the rest."

"You of a mind to tell me your plan? With them two soldiers camping right here in the jail I don't see how you—"

"I don't know either right now, but something's bound to come up. Don't think you ought to know, anyway. Just say you left me in charge of those two soldiers. Up to them to keep me locked up. That way you're not liable to be blamed for me getting away— if I do."

"All right," Fish said. "I'll hang around the Morrals, try to keep them busy—after I bring your horses."

"That'll be a big help, Marshal. And I'm obliged to you for all the favors."

"Only doing what I think's right. Good luck," the lawman said, and crossed to the office area where the two soldiers lounged on the bench. "You boys take it real easy," he said, and moved on through the doorway into the street.

"Hell, there ain't much else we can do," Morgan grumbled. "Sure wish you'd brought them cards."

"Well, I didn't," Davis snapped. "Said you was tired. All right, get some sleep."

Laverty slumped onto his cot. There was nothing to be done but wait—and hope—for the opportunity that would enable him to escape. Such would not be too difficult; the cell was not locked, and he had his gun. The drawbacks were the two soldiers. He'd have to wait until at least one of them dozed off and then—

"Hey, you two bastards!" a voice called cheerfully from the doorway. "Setting there on your arses dogging the duty just like you always do."

"Go to hell, Donohue!" Morgan shot back sourly. He was a squat, dark-haired man with a rugged face heavily seamed by too much whiskey.

"Now, that ain't no way to talk to a bunkie," Donohue chided mildly.

"Where you two headed?" Davis asked, rising and crossing to the door.

"Anyplace where there's some willing women and plenty of drinking liquor," the man with Donohue said.

"Well, you damn better keep your eyes peeled for the lieutenant. He's in town and I expect he's looking to fill the guardhouse."

"That don't bother me none," Donohue said indifferently. "We got passes . . . Come on, Benny, let's go see what's doing at the Eagle."

The two soldiers vanished into the night. Davis pivoted on a heel and came back to his seat on the bench. Nearby Morgan yawned noisily. Out in the street where traces of the day's heat still lingered, there was continuous noise: men shouting, loud laughter, cursing, raucous singing, and the seemingly distant sound of piano music. Somewhere in the far end of the settlement a gunshot flatted through the darkness, bringing a weary comment from Corporal Davis.

"Some other sucker getting hisself killed, I reckon. The colonel's sure going to burn down this goddamn hellhole one of these days, you wait and see."

"Then what'll we do for fun?" Morgan wondered.

"Expect we'll get by. Ain't too far to Wagon Mound."

Tom, restless and on his feet, moved slowly about in his cell. He wished the two soldiers would settle down, that one of them would doze off. Every dragging minute seemed like an hour.

"You recollect that little Mex gal we run into down in Vegas that day?" Davis said.

"Yeh, you bet I do!" Morgan replied. "What about her?"

"I'd sure like to look her up again someday. Keeps me wishing Vegas wasn't so far away. Might get the chance to go there if the colonel ever decides to burn down this collection of garbage bins."

"That ain't likely. I hear he enjoys himself here now and then same as we do—only it's on the sly."

Three more uniformed men appeared in the doorway and voiced their jesting salutations. One, a weasel-faced corporal with shoe-button eyes, grinned broadly.

"Well, howdy-do! Heard you drawed the duty, Davis. Sure pleases me right good to see you cooped up in here, sweating like a field hand, while me and the rest of the troop are in the Castle celebrating big."

Davis did not rise to the taunting bait, merely grumbled something at low breath.

"Well, expect we best be moving on. Sure don't want to keep the ladies waiting," the corporal said, and with his companions moved on.

"Goddamn that Greenleaf," Davis muttered when the party had moved on, "the troop sure was hard up for corporals when they handed him another stripe."

"Don't fret none about that lousy bastard," Morgan said. "We ain't in here forever. The next time we're out on bivouac I'll find a chance to even up with him."

"Expect you'll have to get in line," Davis said, moving toward the cells. "You ain't the only man waiting to get a crack at him."

Tom, sprawled on the cot, closed his eyes and began to breathe deeply, feigning sleep. Davis halted at the end of the cage and studied him briefly, and turned away.

"For a jasper that'll likely be swinging at the end of a rope tomorrow he sure ain't bothered much," the corporal said as he returned to the adjoining room.

Morgan yawned again and got to his feet. "Hell, setting here like this I can't keep my eyes open. I'm going down the street and get myself a drink. Ain't no need for both of us being here anyway."

Davis gave that a bit of thought, then nodded. "All right, go ahead, but keep a sharp eye out for the lieutenant. If he spots you—"

"He won't," Morgan said confidently, crossing to the doorway. "I'll be back in ten, fifteen minutes."

"Just see that it ain't no longer 'n that," Davis said, "and bring back a bottle. Going to get cold in here before morning."

Laverty rose quietly as Davis stretched out on the bench. He'd heard no more from Zack Fish, although he had hoped the lawman would come up with an idea of some sort to help, but he had not and Tom felt he could wait no longer.

Stepping to the cell door, Laverty opened it carefully. He'd need to be out and gone long before Morgan returned. Moving on into the small hallway-like area fronting the cells, Tom drew his gun. Taking it slow and easy, hoping the floor would not creak under his weight, he crossed into the marshal's office. Davis lay with his face turned toward the street.

Tom cast a hurried glance through the doorway. No one was in sight. Grasping the .45 by the barrel, he gave the soldier a sharp blow just below the temple. The corporal groaned softly and went limp. Holstering his weapon, Laverty quickly moved to the doorway and glanced up the street. There were soldiers in the street but none close by—and Morgan was not among them.

Taking a deep breath, Tom stepped out into the cooling night and hurriedly circled the building. There was a slim chance Zack Fish had been able to bring his horses and tie them in the shed. He'd have a look there first.

14

THE shed was a dark bulk some fifty feet away. Tom crossed the distance in long, hurried strides. He swore softly as he drew up to the sagging old structure. It was empty. There had been no real understanding or assurance that the horses would be there after the soldiers had put in their appearance and plans had to be changed, but Laverty felt the possibility had to be checked.

Wheeling, Tom dropped back to the rear of the jail. He had no choice but go to Bellwood's stable himself and chance being recognized by someone along the way.

The street was filled with noise. A dust pall hung in the air, and a dozen or more men could be seen, some lounging around the fronts of the saloons, others simply wandering about. A few women were in evidence, all gaudily dressed and usually in the company of three or four soldiers. A uniformed figure sprawled in the shadow of a nearby building, drunk or dead, while the strains of "Believe Me If All Those Endearing Young Charms" drifted through the open doorway of King's Castle to be quickly lost in the confusion of laughter and shouting.

Halting at the edge of the jail, Laverty glanced down the street and located Bellwood's stable. It would be impossible to reach it without being noticed by someone—thanks to Nate Gilmore, who had created a host of enemies for him.

Pivoting, Tom hurried to the rear of the building, hopeful of finding an alley. He had little time, he realized. Davis would soon recover his senses, and Morgan, his thirst satisfied, would be returning to the jail.

There was an area behind the first building littered with trash that he could cross. Laverty, now moving at a run, covered the distance behind that structure and the two that lay beyond. There he came to a halt. The next building, King's Castle, blocked what served as an alley with the small shacks provided for the women. A fence to their left further closed off any advance in that direction. He had no choice but to go back to the street and take his chances on being recognized.

There was no time to think about the problem and the danger it posed. Pulling his hat low, Tom moved at a quick pace along the side of the Castle, fairly rocking with sound, and reached the street. Turning left, he paused. The door of the saloon was open, and just inside, sitting at a table with the Morrals, Gilmore, and two other men was Town Marshal Fish.

Laverty wasted no time wondering what was being said by the men, but it did explain what had happened to the lawman and why he'd heard no more from him.

Tom frowned as he crossed the front of the saloon and stepped down into the alleyway, which separated it from the next building where two men, observed by a small circle of observers, were slugging it out in the semidarkness. Had Zack Fish double-crossed him?

Had the lawman, in the interest of keeping his job as marshal, or for some other reason, changed his thinking and lined up with the Morrals, or Nate Gilmore?

It appeared to be just that, Tom thought grimly as he hurried on through the dusty darkness. Evidently Fish had told the saloon man and the Morrals that he was safe in jail being guarded by two soldiers, and the question to be solved was who was to have first choice; the Morrals because he had killed their brother, or Gilmore and the merchants, who hoped to smooth things over with the Army by hanging him.

Laverty grinned tightly as he turned down another weedy and trash-filled corridor lying between two buildings and hurried toward what appeared in the half-light to be the alley he had been following earlier. His assumption proved to be correct, and moving fast along the cluttered strip, the sounds coming from the saloons and other houses as well as in the street filling his ears, he continued on until he had reached the rear of Bellwood's stable.

The wide door was open and, entering, Tom made his way through the darkness to the runway. A lantern hanging just inside the front entrance guided him along the wide strip that bisected the stable and, moving silently, he hurried to the forward end of the building.

There appeared to be no one on duty, which was not unusual. At night most stable owners turned their business over to a hostler, who could be counted on to be sleeping during the late hours, or else periodically took time off to go get himself a drink. However, there was the possibility the man was somewhere in the stable, perhaps reading or dozing, and taking no chances, Laverty continued to move quietly.

He located the bay gelding in the third stall, the pack horse in the fourth. His gear had been slung over the intervening wall and, working fast, he first saddled and bridled the bay and then moved to where the buckskin was tethered. It took but a few minutes to put the pack saddle, still loaded, in place. When the horses were ready, he backed them into the runway and led them to the rear opening of the stable.

Reaching the doorway, Tom swung onto the bay, a feeling of relief coming over him as tension began to drain from his taut shape. He was again on his horse; he was once more free, and he was leaving Pardo— the town called Sodom on the Mora—behind him.

Pointing the bay straight ahead, Laverty raked the big gelding lightly with his spurs and put him into a slow trot. Follow the river north; such would lead him to Colorado and eventually to Cheyenne, Zack Fish had said. Tom gave that thought. If the lawman had gone over to the side of the merchants, or the Morrals, he perhaps should strike out in a different direction.

Fish would assume he'd head north as planned and, if a posse was formed, lead it up the river.

Laverty came to the Mora, and the need for a decision was at hand. He hesitated there for a long minute, eyes on the silvery, glistening water. He'd have a good start on any posse and the odds for escaping one would all be in his favor. Anyway, where else could he go but south—the way he had come—and that would be a foolish move. He'd go on, head for Cheyenne, and take his chances on eluding a posse or anyone else who appeared on his back trail.

He was now a fugitive from the law—an outlaw, Laverty realized—and that would mean he must avoid lawmen. Of course it would be a few days before word got around, but as vengeful as Gilmore and the other merchants of Pardo were, he could expect the day to come when every sheriff and marshal in that part of the country would be on the lookout for him. And he shouldn't sell the Morrals short; sooner or later, he was bound to hear from them.

Maybe once he reached Cheyenne he should just keep on going, forget about heading back to Arizona and Madden's ranch. It just might be smart to go on into Dakota Territory or even Montana. He'd heard both were good cattle country and big ranches were plentiful. He could find himself a job in one or the other, and be handy to the Canadian border if the law came looking for him.

Riding along the narrow, shining river, which murmured softly as it flowed over its rocky bed, Tom glanced back over his shoulder toward the town. In the distance it was no more than a lighted bubble of dust from which issued faint sounds of activity.

Surely Davis and Morgan had raised an alarm by that time. Like as not they had hurried along the street in search of him first and, failing, had then set out to locate Lieutenant Joseph and give him the bad news of his escape—a dereliction of duty that was certain to earn them some time in the guardhouse.

He wouldn't have heard the alarm if it had taken place while he was getting his horses because of the noise in the street, so he had no idea of how soon he could expect riders on his trail. Not for a while, he hoped, as he moved steadily on through the low hill country. He'd like to reach the first settlement Zack Fish had mentioned—Ocate Crossing, he thought it was. Once there he'd take stock of his situation, for likely Ocate Crossing would be the last place he'd have a chance to change his mind about going to Cheyenne or points farther north.

Hours earlier, on the trail that followed the Mora River north, Lou Petty drew the mare to a halt and slid from the saddle. She groaned as her feet struck the ground, and pain laced through her legs and back. Lou was no stranger to riding a horse, but never before had she stayed in the saddle so long or ridden so hard. A half hour, at the most an hour, was about the duration of her usual rides.

Moving slowly to the stream, Lou squatted down

and bathed her face with the cold water. Nearby the sorrel took advantage of the moment and slaked her thirst.

There had been no one following her, Lou was certain of that, as she had taken the precaution to stop on the rises now and then and study the moonlit country behind her. Of course John King and some of his hired help, if they were pursuing her, could take the trouble to keep out of sight in the brush and trees that bordered the trail, but even so it seemed likely she would have caught a glimpse of them at one time or another.

Luck could be with her, Lou thought, taking up the reins of the mare and starting on up the trail on foot. It was about time; she hadn't known any real good luck since meeting John King that day in Dodge City.

She had just gone to work in one of the saloons as a calico girl waiting on tables, and nothing else, when King had introduced himself. He told her of his fine place in Pardo, which he said was near a fort, and proceeded to paint a glowing picture of an easy life where much money could be made.

She had fallen for his line and, quitting her job, gone on to Pardo with him. Shortly after arriving, Lou learned she was to be nothing more than a bed slave to him, and one he would not hesitate to rent out as long as the prospective customer could pay the price.

Those first days were a terrible experience and Lou shuddered as she recalled them. King did not hesitate to beat her cruelly if she displeased him or went against his wishes, and it soon became prudent to do

as he told her if she did not want to suffer the conse-
quences.

Several times she had considered running away, but
on each occasion her determination had withered
when she thought of what would happen if she failed
to escape. Other women working for John King had
tried, only to be brought back by King and his hired
hands—two dark, muscular Mexican men who took
delight in manhandling their charges when King was
not around.

But Lou had never given up the hope of one day
being free of King, and somehow the words she'd had
with Tom Laverty seemed to crystallize her hope and
determination, and she had made up her mind that the
time to try had come. The money she had saved, however little, plus the gold eagles her father had sent,
provided her with a fair stake, one that should enable
her—assuming she escaped King—to make a clean
start in some far-distant town.

Lou hadn't decided yet just where that would be, but
it should be somewhere far from Pardo. She halted,
stood for a time fingering the cameo locket that hung
around her neck. Cheyenne was where Tom Laverty
had been headed for when he ran into trouble; maybe
that would be a good place for her, too.

And it just could be she'd run into him somewhere
along the way. Marshal Fish was going to turn him
loose, probably had already done so. A half smile
formed on her lips. She wouldn't mind it a bit having
him riding at her side all the way to Wyoming.

15

NATE GILMORE, hard features pulled into an angry scowl, considered the men sitting at the table with him. Besides Town Marshal Fish there were the two Morral brothers, who were steadily soaking up whiskey like a dry creek bed absorbs water, general-store owner Ned Hazlett, saloon man Angus Dolittle, and Dave Shortle, who operated the White Rose bawdy house.

Standing close by were restaurant owner Pete Willoughby, Todd Calgary of Calgary's Gun Shop, three interested patrons of the Castle, and John King himself.

"Still claim what I'm saying we do is best," Gilmore declared, raising his voice to be heard above the noise in the Castle. Several couples were engaged in stomp dancing, the thud of their heels on the floor all but drowning out the piano. "Be the only way we'll ever satisfy that colonel."

Ben Morral shook his head as he twirled the shot glass of liquor before him between a thumb and forefinger. His coarse features were set and his colorless eyes were like agates.

"Nope, he belongs to me and Charlie. Was our kin he shot down," he said in a stubborn, rough-edged voice. "Ain't you or the Army or nobody else going to finagle us out of our just due."

"That's right," Charlie Morral said, refilling his

glass, "he's ourn!"

"I ain't saying you don't have a call," Gilmore continued, "but we've got to consider the town. That colonel out at the fort means business this time, and unless we do something real quick to satisfy him, every place in Pardo could go up in smoke."

"He's right, Ben," John King said, glancing off to the left where a fight had broken out. "We can't afford to bring the Army down on us—"

"I would've had the whole mess settled by now if it hadn't been for the marshal there," Gilmore broke in, pointing an accusing finger at Fish.

"Nate's right!" one of the bystanders, who had apparently been a member of Gilmore's lynch mob earlier, said. "We had a rope and was all set to hang him when the marshal butted in."

The brawl over near the roulette wheel ended as abruptly as it had started, and the dancing had ceased and was being replaced by a woman singing in a high, quavery voice.

"Man was my prisoner," the lawman said defensively. "Ain't nobody ever took a prisoner away from me and I weren't about to let it start now."

"Could have saved us all a lot of trouble if you'd just turned your back and let Nate and the others have their way," Willoughby, a tall, spare man with a cigar butt clamped between his teeth, commented sourly.

"And we could've easy got the job done if Fish there hadn't made that killer a deputy and give him back his gun."

The speaker's words were barely audible through the din that now filled the saloon. The woman had finished her song and dancing was again under way. A loud argument was going on at the table next to the one where the meeting was taking place, and abruptly Ben Morral, anger suddenly overflowing, jerked out his gun and fired two quick shots into the ceiling. As the echoes rocked around the room and smoke billowed upward to mix with that from the oil lamps hanging like a storm cloud over the room, Morral glared at those around him.

"Cut out all that goddamn racket! A man can't hear hisself break wind!" he shouted, and turned his attention back to the bystander. "What was that you was saying about that killer being a deputy?"

"Said the marshal made him one—swore him in. We could've handled Fish there, him carrying just the old scattergun of his, but that other bird, he had a six-gun, and we all had seen how good he was with it when he shot Kurt. We wasn't about to buck him."

"That true, Marshal?" Todd Calgary asked.

The lawman nodded.

"Why in God's name would you do that?" Calgary continued in a shocked voice. "He'd just killed a man, was facing a murder charge. Can't see why—"

"In the first place the man was only defending himself against Kurt," Fish said. "I've got a dozen witnesses who'll testify to that."

"Maybe," Charlie Morral said pointedly. "Just maybe they'd speak up against us."

The saloon had returned to its original state of loud talking, laughter, men shouting back and forth, and noisy dancing. Chair legs scraped on the floor, and over in one corner there was the shattering of glass as someone, for some reason, overturned a table.

"Point is, what're we going to do now? He's locked up with a couple of soldiers from the fort standing guard over him. Are we going ahead and take the law into our own hands or are we just going to set by and let the Army tell us what's what?"

Gilmore shook his head at Shortle. "Way I understand it, the Army ain't planning to do anything about it other 'n see that we do something."

"Meaning the colonel's leaving it up to us."

"Yes, sir; and if we don't handle it to suit him, then he aims to step in, and you know what that means."

"Hell, he ain't about to burn us out," Calgary said. "Them soldier boys've got to have someplace to go."

"He could close us down for a spell," Hazlett said, rubbing at the stubble on his jaw. "Sure would hate that."

"We all would," John King said, his attention on two men tussling with one of the saloon girls near the door to his combination office and quarters. "You men decide what ought to be done. I'll go along with it whatever it is," he added, and turning, hurried toward the disturbance.

Gilmore followed the saloon man with his eyes for a few moments, and then shrugged. "King sure don't like anybody roughing up his women . . . Now, let's get back to the problem. We've got to do something before the colonel gets here in the morning."

"I don't see what all the hurry is," Ned Hazlett said with a shake of his head. "Be all the same if we wait for him and let him watch us try the man and then hang him."

"That won't be half as effective as if we'd already held a trial, convicted, and strung him up," Gilmore insisted. "He'd know then we mean business when it comes to shootings, and are doing our level best to keep killers out of Pardo."

Ben Morral turned his head, spat on the floor. "You all keep forgetting one thing," he said lazily. "Me and Charlie've got first dibs on that bird—Laverty or whatever his name is. You're just flapping your jaws."

"Anybody seen Lieutenant Joseph?" a voice called from the bar. "Corporal here says their prisoner's gone and escaped."

"Escaped!" Gilmore yelled, leaping to his feet. He pointed at one of the soldiers speaking to the bartender. "You one of the men they left to guard Laverty?"

The corporal nodded. "The lieutenant posted Private Morgan and me to guard him, but there was something wrong with the deal. The prisoner had a gun and the key to his cell."

"Now how in the hell did he get his hands on them?" Ben Morral demanded, his face flushed with anger. "Just how?"

"Only thing I can figure is he had them all the time, like maybe the marshal give them to him."

Morral and the others turned their attention to the lawman. John King, who had come up a few moments earlier, stared at the lawman.

"What about it, Marshal? You give that killer his gun and the key to his cell?"

Fish shrugged. "Reckon I plain forgot to take them back after I made him a deputy."

"Forgot!" Calgary exploded. "Just what kind of a jail are you running, Zack?"

"One I say we'd best lock him up in," Gilmore said. "My guess is that Laverty paid him off to let him go or else he's hand in glove with that killer. Big thing is we've got to have somebody to show the colonel in the morning." Nate paused, glanced at the corporal. "You got any idea which way Laverty went when he got away?"

"Nope, sure ain't," the non-com replied. "Said he was going to Cheyenne when he was talking to Lou Petty and Kurt. Likely headed that way now."

"Lou was talking to him?" King asked, frowning.

"Sure was. Said he had something for her, and needed to talk to her a bit . . . What're we going to do about the marshal?"

"Lock him up; we'll trade him off to the colonel, tell him we're holding him responsible for the killer getting away," Calgary said. "Except the next thing is to get a posse together and go after Laverty."

"Count me in on it," King said. "Just found out Lou Petty has run off. I've got a hunch she's with him."

"That's a good bet," Gilmore agreed. "Now how many of—"

"Forget about that posse," Ben Morral said, pushing back from the table and getting to his feet. "Me and Charlie'll go after him."

"I'll ride with you," King said. "Take a little time to get a posse together, and I want to catch up with her fast as I can."

Gilmore, frowning, was studying the Morral brothers thoughtfully. "Can we figure on you bringing him back here so's we can hold a trial and hang him all legal-like?"

Ben laughed humorlessly. "Can figure on us bringing him back, all right. Can't say whether he'll be in any shape to stand trial."

Gilmore considered that for a few moments and then smiled wanly. "Well, I reckon it won't make much difference, so long as he don't get away and we end up making that colonel happy . . . you two and King go up the river. I'll get some men together and cut across to the trail. That way we'll have him sort of boxed in."

Ben shrugged his thick shoulders and winked at Charlie, now on his feet and standing nearby. "Suit yourself," he said, and started for the door with his brother at his heels. Midway, Morral slowed and glanced back to King. "If you're riding with us, get your horse and meet us at the bridge in ten minutes, else we'll be going on without you."

"I'll be there," King said, lean features taut and dark eyes filled with anger. "You can count on it."

Ben nodded and, with the burly Charlie now ahead of him, moved on. Gilmore turned to the men remaining at the table and to a larger group gathered around it. The two soldiers had disappeared, evidently having gone in search of the lieutenant. He glanced at Zack Fish.

"First thing we got to do is lock up the marshal, then we'll be ready to ride. All of you aiming to come along meet me at the jail as soon as you get your horses and gear."

16

THE night was cool, and a near-full moon brightened the hills about Tom and made following the trail along the river easy. About him the weeds and grass were alive with the sounds of small animals and insects, and birds stirred nervously at his passage. Not too far off, on the slopes of the mountains to the east, coyotes wailed, and somewhere behind him a lone wolf voiced an eerie challenge.

He had passed the Adams place, a two-storied wood and stone structure, along with a few small houses, all of which were in total darkness, the latter appearing to have been abandoned. As he hurried on, pressing the horses to maintain a steady lope, Laverty had but one thing in mind: to be as far from Pardo as possible by first light and still not punish the bay and the buckskin or take chances when they were on uncertain footing. Without a horse he would be in much deeper trouble and he was not about to risk that.

Several times he halted on a crest to breathe the animals, taking advantage of the pause to study his back trail for signs of pursuit. He could see clearly for a considerable distance, and not once was there any indication of riders following him.

That puzzled Laverty to some extent. It was only logical to think a posse headed by Gilmore and the other merchants, who sought his blood as a sop to the commander at the fort, would be out to recapture him. And it was possible that Town Marshal Fish, protecting his job, could be counted among them—not to mention the possibility of the Army sending out a patrol to assist in running him down.

They would know he intended to head north. He had mentioned it earlier in the Castle when he tried to talk with Lou Petty. That could explain why there was no one in pursuit, he concluded after a time; Gilmore might be thinking that he had swung over to the Santa Fe Trail cutoff, and a posse, if there was one—and Tom was certain there was—was following it.

Such wouldn't be the case, however, if Zack Fish were in charge. The lawman had told him to follow the river if he intended to go north, and that's what he had done.

He reckoned he owed Zack Fish. The marshal had been the only one in town to recognize the truth about the shoot-out with Kurt Morral, and had stood by him against Nate Gilmore and his lynching party when they had come after him earlier that night. Zack had jeopardized his job as town marshal when he did it, and had further endangered his position by making an escape possible—whether accidentally or intentionally Tom was still uncertain.

Zack had left him on his own, armed and with the key to his cell, which was actually unlocked, while he went off, ostensibly to keep an eye on the Morral brothers. Escaping the soldiers left to guard him had been easy, but as he was hurrying to get his horses he had seen the marshal with Gilmore, the Morrals, and several others in King's saloon, deep in conversation. Was the lawman simply keeping Gilmore and the others busy or was he there making plans for the coming day when Laverty would be tried and hanged for the shooting of Kurt Morral?

The problem troubled Laverty as he rode on. Zack Fish struck him as a fair and honest man, one who would stand by his convictions and his word. And Tom had to admit that he had no real proof that the lawman had double-crossed him. He could have been in King's Castle doing what he could to keep Gilmore and the others tied down—and not making plans for the hanging that Gilmore was so anxious to put on for the benefit of the Fort Union commander. For the time being he'd give Zack the best of it, and simply assume the lawman had not crossed him up.

The trail, now just two parallel ruts in the rocky soil, began to curve east and swing away from the stream. Fish had said to follow the river, and the trail's gradual departure from it aroused a slight worry in Laverty.

But he was still bearing north according to the stars and that was the direction he knew he must maintain. Somewhere on ahead was a settlement called Ocate Crossing. Beyond it were a couple more, after which a town called Raton and the Colorado line. Once he reached this, he'd have it made.

The country about him was also gradually changing. The mountains off to his left appeared higher and well covered with trees—pines, Tom thought. The ground yet had its blanket of grass and shrubbery was plentiful, but the big, spreading cottonwoods remained by the river.

It was around three o'clock, Tom judged, when he reached the settlement of Ocate Crossing and pulled off into the brush at one side. Expecting a town of at least a dozen houses with a general store and saloon, he was disappointed to find only a couple of aged and weathered huts. There was no sign of life, which was understandable considering the hour, but he had thought there would be horses to see, perhaps cattle and almost certainly a dog to herald his arrival. There was nothing other than a ghostly silence. Any supplies he needed and had hoped to buy there would have to be obtained elsewhere.

Laverty allowed the horses to rest and water by the stream that crossed the trail a short distance beyond the settlement, and then pressed on. The next place, he recalled Zack Fish saying, was Rayado, some fifteen miles farther on, but whether it was actually a town or not Tom now had doubts. Ocate Crossing, if he had seen all of it, certainly was not, which, when he thought of it, was probably a good thing. A posse following him up the river would halt there and ask about his passing. No one in Ocate Crossing would be able to report his having been there.

He would have to stop soon, however, make camp, eat a little, and let the horses rest. They had come a far distance in a fairly short time since leaving Pardo, and had done so at a steady pace. It was fortunate they had enjoyed a good feeding of grain and a few hours' rest in Bellwood's stable, otherwise they could not have done so well. But there was a limit to their strength and endurance as well as his own. Rayado was only couple of hours farther on; he'd push on until he reached it.

He came in sight of the place an hour or so after first light. It proved to be little more than its name denoted: a crossing as near as he could tell, and looked to be either a ranch or trading post. Laverty gave it thought, decided he could do without the supplies he needed until he reached a more sizable settlement where he would draw less attention. That would be Cimarron, he reckoned, and veering off the trail toward a peaked mountain rising high above the surrounding country, he drew in beside a small creek and halted.

First picketing the horses where they had both grass and water, Tom unloaded his sack of grub as well as the one containing necessary cooking utensils, built a fire, and put a pot of coffee on to boil. Digging into his supplies, he found several biscuits, some almost rancid bacon, a few potatoes, and a somewhat dried-out onion.

Chunking the bacon into a skillet, he placed it over the fire while he cut the potatoes and onion into thin slices. Adding them to the now-sizzling bacon, he set several of the biscuits to warming on top of the mixture in the spider and then leaned back. Shortly the coffee surged to the top of the pot, rattling the lid noisily, and removing it from the fire, he stirred down the froth with his knife, took up a cup, and poured himself a measure of the steaming, black brew. After the first swallow his spirits revived and he felt better. It came to him then that he had not eaten since—

"What the hell are you doing here" a voice demanded harshly from the nearby brush.

Startled, Laverty remained motionless for several moments. It couldn't be the posse, he was certain; they wouldn't have asked any questions. Setting down his cup, he turned slowly to see the speaker.

"Fixing to eat."

"You picked the wrong place, drifter!" The rider was a lean, hawk-faced man in range clothing. He had a rifle cradled in the crook of his arm, and not far behind him was a second rider similarly armed. Their horses were a few yards farther on, which accounted for the noiseless approach of the pair. "You're on private range. The boss don't allow no trespassing."

"Was following the trail along the river. Nothing private about that," Tom said coolly as he drew himself erect.

"You ain't on the river now! This here's Marshfield range, the trail's over east of here a ways. That's where you damn pilgrims are supposed to be, not here messing up a man's grass and maybe starting a range fire. Now, load up and move on."

Tom suppressed his anger. "My horses are beat. So am I. I'll move out soon as we've rested a mite," he said, and hand resting lightly on the butt of his gun, turned slightly to face the two men squarely.

"He ain't doing no harm, Ed," the second rider said. "Can't see no reason why he can't finish his eating and resting."

Ed frowned, spat. "Damn it, Arnie, you know what Mr. Marshfield said about trespassing."

"Way I see it he ain't exactly trespassing. Probably got on that old road down the Crossing somewhere and just followed it north. It ain't his fault the boss never got around to blocking it off."

Ed pulled off his hat and ran his fingers through his hair as he considered his partner's words. Then his bony shoulders stirred.

"I reckon it'll be all right this time, but you get yourself over to the trail, and you be damn sure that fire's out! We've had enough range go up in smoke already this year to last for a long spell. Where you headed!"

"North."

"Expect you're meaning Colorado. Just get on the trail and follow your nose," Ed snapped, and wheeling about, rejoined his partner.

Dropping to a crouch again, Tom watched the pair

ride off as he stirred the mixture in the spider with his knife. He hadn't realized he was so close to the trail that the merchant in Watrous had spoken about, and it didn't please him. A posse following him could take that well-traveled route, but there was nothing to do about it at that moment, he decided, turning his attention back to the skillet. The bacon was done but the potatoes and onion were still hard, he saw as he set the warmed biscuits off to one side.

Maybe he should cross over and get on the trail, he thought, taking up his cup of coffee again. If a posse were following him up the river at the direction of Zack Fish, his being on the trail, which he had been paralleling since leaving Pardo, might just confuse them and get them off his back. Of course, if there were two posses, only one of which had followed the trail, such a move would be risky.

No, despite cowhand Ed's warning, he'd keep riding north on the old trail that he had been following, Laverty decided, setting the spider off the fire and taking up one of the biscuits. He'd be a lot safer there where there was plenty of brush and trees to ride through; along the Santa Fe Trail, after years of use, there most likely would be little growth left to afford a man cover.

Reaching into the grub sack, Tom located a spoon and, squatting on his haunches, dipped it into the delicious-smelling stewlike concoction in the skillet. He'd make short work of—

"Tom? Tom Laverty?"

17

IT was a woman's voice, one vaguely familiar. Laverty pivoted, swore softly. It was Lou Petty, as she called herself. She was standing at the edge of the brush on ahead a short distance.

"I was hoping it was you," the woman said, smiling as she hurried toward him. "I took your advice."

Laverty frowned, resumed his eating. "Advice?"

"You told me I should quit the life I was leading, take the money Papa sent and start over somewhere else."

Lou had changed from her gay saloon-girl clothing, was now clad in more sensible attire for the trail: men's pants, shirt, high-top shoes, and woolen jacket. She had a red scarf tied about her head to which she had added a short-brimmed hat.

"You eat yet?" he asked, noting her eyes on the skillet.

"Yes, some, but whatever you're cooking certainly smells good. I—"

Tom reached into the gunny sack in which he carried utensils and produced a plate, a spoon, and another cup. Dipping out a generous measure of the stew onto the plate and adding one of the biscuits, he handed it to her.

"Coffee's there, ready when you want it."

Lou accepted the plate with a smile and sat down near the fire. "Thank you," she murmured.

Tom continued his breakfasting and for a time no words passed between him and the woman, but when the last of the food was gone and each had settled back with a second cup of coffee, Laverty put his attention on her. She was prettier without the cosmetics she had affected, and looked much younger. Too, her eyes seemed bluer and what was visible of her dark hair had a faint reddish tinge in the morning sunlight.

"Expect you've made up your mind where you're going," he said, taking a sip of the now-cool coffee.

Lou's thick brows lifted. "I thought I'd go on to Cheyenne with you—if it's all right?"

Laverty did not look up. He wasn't pleased with the idea of having a woman on his hands, particularly when he wasn't certain of what lay ahead where the Morrals and the possibility of posses were concerned. But the girl needed help; she would have a hard time making it to Cheyenne alone.

"I reckon it'll be all right," he said, finishing off the coffee and setting the cup aside. Reaching into his shirt pocket, he produced his cigarette makings.

Lou watched him roll a smoke and then, as he started to put the sack of tobacco and fold of papers away, she extended her hand toward him.

"Mind if I make myself a cigarette, too?"

At first Tom was surprised, but a moment later he realized he was not dealing with the girl he had envisioned as the daughter of Henry Pettibone but with Lou Petty, a woman wise to the ways of the harder kind of life. Nodding, he passed the makings to her.

"I was actually waiting for you," she said frankly as she expertly rolled a slim cylinder of tobacco and paper between her long fingers. "I remembered you saying you were headed for Cheyenne, and I figured you'd be coming this way."

"Took a chance there; I could have gone over and got on the trail."

"Yes, you could have," Lou said, returning the tobacco and packet of brown papers to him, "but I doubt it. Everybody around Pardo follows the road along the river when they go to Cimarron. They get on the trail there if they're headed north. It's shorter, they say. You save a few miles unless you intend to go east."

Tom struck a match and lit her cigarette. "Don't know much about the country, just what I've been told. Zack Fish said to follow the river and that's what I did."

"It was good of him to let you go," Lou said, puffing the cigarette into life and nodding her thanks.

Laverty shrugged. "Not sure that he did, but I owe him some thanks anyway. Wouldn't be here right now if he hadn't left me my gun and the door to my cell open . . . You wait long for me?"

"Stopped at Ocate Crossing first, thinking you'd be along right away; I heard the marshal say he was letting you go. When you didn't show up, I thought it best to move on, stop farther on up the river."

He looked at her closely. "King after you?"

"I expect so—if he has found out I've gone," she

replied, letting smoke trickle out the corners of her mouth.

"What right's he got to make you stay if you want to leave?"

"John King thinks he owns every girl that works for him. They never leave unless he wants to get rid of them."

Laverty grinned wryly. "Appears we're both in a bad way. King's looking for you, the Morrals would like to shoot me for killing their brother, and half the town's out to catch me and string me up to please that colonel at the fort. Expect you're sorry by now that you ran away from your folks," Laverty added as he began to collect the pans and dishes.

"No, I'll never regret that," Lou said flatly, pitching in to help. "Being a preacher's daughter was no life for me. We lived on handouts—food, clothes, everything. I never saw any money because there simply wasn't any. The people Pa ministered to were almost as poor as we were—poor as Job's turkey, he used to say—and I think he took a kind of pride in us being that way."

They had collected the utensils and were walking over to the creek to clean them.

"I hated to go to school. There was always some girl there who'd point to the dress I was wearing and tell everybody that it once was hers or her ma's or maybe an older sister's. Maybe you think I was wrong to leave home, but the truth is I just couldn't stand it there any longer."

Tom shook his head as he knelt by the stream and scrubbed the frying pan with the sand and water. "Make it a rule to never judge anybody when it comes to their problems," he said, and as they finished the washing, added: "Where's your horse?"

"I left her over there behind that thicket. I wasn't sure it was you I heard coming."

Tom handed her the skillet and other dishes they had washed. "Take these and put them in the gunny sack— not the flour sack with the grub in it, but the one with other pans in it. I'll get your horse."

Lou frowned. "You think the men following you— us—are getting close?"

"Could be. Only smart we keep moving."

He found Lou's horse, a sleek little sorrel, behind the brush she had pointed out, noting with satisfaction as he approached the mare that the woman seemed to have come well prepared. There was a blanket roll and a slicker tied to the saddle, and the leather bags hanging across its skirt were bulging with trail necessities and what he assumed was grub.

Taking up the lines, he led the sorrel back to where his horses were picketed. He waited there for a time while the sorrel drank, and then brought all three to the camp. Lou had just finished storing the utensils.

"I guess we'd best fill the canteens," she said, pouring what coffee was left in the pot onto the fire.

Tom nodded, and taking the container from her saddle, he hung his over his shoulder and dropped back to the stream. Filling them quickly, he again retraced his steps, pleased when he reached there to find Lou had everything in readiness to travel.

Hanging her canteen on the horn of the sorrel's saddle, he moved on to where the bay waited and mounted. As he secured his water container he glanced at the woman. She was already on the sorrel.

"I don't think it's too far from here to the next town, one called Cimarron," he said. "Need to stop there and get some grub. Then we can make a run for Colorado."

Lou looked over her shoulder as they moved out. "You'll be all right once we cross over and get into a different territory. The law can't touch you then. But that won't stop John King."

Laverty shrugged. "Long as I'm around, he won't bother you—if that's what you want."

"Thank you, Tom," the woman said. "That's what I want."

SHE was glad she had waited for Tom Laverty. At first she had halted at Ocate Crossing and was prepared to stay there, but after an hour or so when he had not put in his appearance, the fear of being overtaken by John King had possessed her and she'd ridden on, staying in the saddle until she was too weary to go any farther.

Halting in the trees and brush somewhere past Rayado, she had climbed off the mare and almost without bothering to unroll the blankets, had lain down and slept for a time. When she awoke the sun was up.

Anxiety had again gripped her. By pulling off the trail and dozing off, she had no doubt allowed Tom Laverty to pass her by. Hurriedly rolling her blankets and wrapping the slicker about them, she restored them to their place behind the cantle of her saddle and mounted the mare. At that moment she heard the voice of a man. It wasn't Laverty, she was sure, and mindful of the danger a woman alone on the trail incurred, she dismounted and, leaving the sorrel well hidden, made her way to where she could look out into the small clearing lying to the east.

It was Laverty. He was hunched by a small fire cooking his breakfast. Two men faced him from a bit farther on and one was speaking to Tom in a hard voice, evidently demanding that he move on. Lou could not catch all the words being spoken, but she guessed Tom was being accused of trespassing and ordered to move on.

If such was the case, Laverty was not being very cooperative. He continued to prepare whatever it was he had in a skillet, and after a time the two cowhands walked back to their horses and rode off.

A faint smile came to her lips at that, for it was exactly the way Tom Laverty affected people. In his quiet, confident manner he had apparently told the cowhands he would move on when he was ready to do so, and the man, evidently deeming it unwise to press things any further—and rightly so—had let it go at that.

Tom Laverty was a real man, the kind she had

always dreamed of meeting and someday marrying. But she doubted Tom would ever entertain such ideas where she was concerned, knowing what she was and the sort of life she'd led.

But you'd never know that from the way he treated her. He was polite, courteous, and understanding, just as if she were one of those high-toned, quality ladies that she had read about in the magazines.

She had called out to him at that point, and he had turned to face her. His surprise was evident, but he had welcomed her nevertheless and agreed to her riding with him the rest of the way to Cheyenne.

That he would protect her from John King, and men like him, Laverty had made clear, but almost before he had spoken words to that effect, Lou had begun to hope for something more meaningful.

18

THE morning was a cool one, and quite pleasant. Horned larks flitted up from the grass-covered land ahead of the horses as they loped steadily along, and off to the left a considerable distance a band of antelope, their white rumps shining in the sunlight, raced off in fright. In the distance to the west, the towering, snowcapped peaks of the Sangre de Cristo Mountains glistened against the blue sky.

Reaching a sharp rise in the flat across which they were moving, Laverty, doubly wary now of pursuit, twisted about and had a long, searching look at the trail behind them.

"Do you see anybody?" Lou asked anxiously.

Tom settled back in his saddle and shook his head. "Nope, nobody; but that's no guarantee there ain't. They could be smart enough to do their riding in the brush, out of sight."

"Too, they could be coming up the trail," Lou said. "The roads all kind of come together up here somewhere."

"Good chance there's two posses," Tom said, agreeing. "One could be following the road along the river, the other on the trail. Army could be around somewhere, too. I reckon it all depends on how bad they want me."

"And me," Lou said. "King will be with one of them. He's sure to figure we'll be together."

Laverty studied her quiet features for a bit. "About time King learned that slavery ended with the War between the States," he said. "He's got no right to keep you working for him if you don't want to."

"John King makes his own laws when it comes to the Castle. The way he sees it, he not only owns the place but the girls and everything else that's in it."

"Is it the same with the rest of the saloon owners?"

"Some—and where a lot of the girls are concerned, they like it that way. Means they always have a job and don't ever have to worry about a place to sleep or where their next meal is coming from. Some of them will stay right there until they die."

"Not much of a life," Laverty said as they moved on.

Lou was silent, seemingly occupied by the country through which they were passing: a series of low hills, arroyos, and reddish bluffs.

"I guess it all depends on what you came from," she said after a time. "Most of the girls I knew were like me: running away from something, hoping to leave something behind, and taking a job in a saloon was the only thing they could find to do. Out in this part of the country there's not much else for a woman."

Laverty murmured his agreement, eyes now on two riders well to the east and traveling north at a good pace. The Morrals? There were two of them, which made this notion feasible, but the distance was too great for any identification. Also, they could be members of a posse, one assembled by Nate Gilmore, assuming he got one together, but if so could they have caught up with him so soon?

Whoever they were, he'd best keep them in mind until he knew for certain who they were. Like as not they were only a couple of pilgrims or cowhands headed for Cimarron just as he and Lou Petty—but he'd not take that for granted.

"That fellow—Kurt Morral—he mean something special to you?"

Interest stirred through Lou. "No—why?"

"Well, you were sitting there at that table with him and that other jasper—"

"That was Jess Farley. He is, or was, Kurt's best friend."

"Thought maybe Morral meant something to you

the way you were acting."

"Like he might be a man I would marry? I should say not! I hated Kurt just like I hate Ben and Charlie Morral. They're all trash—brutes."

"Then what were you doing with him? Any woman in any saloon I ever knew could pick and choose who she wanted to be with."

"Not if they worked for John King. He favored the Morrals because they spent a lot of money in the Castle. And for some reason they all took a fancy to me. King saw that, and every time they came in he pushed me off on them."

Laverty nodded. "I see."

Lou leaned slightly forward in her saddle and looked closely at Tom. In the bright light of day, the blue of her eyes took on a different shade.

"Why? Is there some special reason why you want to know?" A thin thread of hope was running through Lou's voice as if she sought some evidence of his having more than a protective interest in her.

"No, just asking," Laverty said laconically. "Sure wouldn't like it much if I'd killed the man you aimed to marry."

Lou straightened in her saddle, lips now turned down in disappointment. "I'd never marry a man like Kurt Morral," she said, and then added: "Chances are I'll never get any man to marry me once he knows what I've been."

"Doubt if that'll matter much to a man who finds himself caring enough to want you for his wife."

"I hope you're right, Tom," she said quietly. "I never thought before to ask, but are you married? I just assumed—"

"Nope, never seemed to have the time. Reckon I would be, though, if I'd ever run into the right girl."

"Well, I hope you find her someday," Lou said, staring straight ahead across the grassy plain they were approaching. "Don't you need some sleep?"

"No, caught a few winks while I was in jail, then done a bit in the saddle as I was going along the river. Never been one to need much shut-eye."

"The same with me, but I am getting drowsy now. I guess it's the quiet and the warm sun. This is so different from working in the Castle. I seldom got outside except to walk from my cabin to the saloon—or maybe go to the store for something."

"King's Castle the only saloon you ever worked in?"

"No, there's been a couple of others—starting with Dodge City."

"Been there once. They called it Buffalo City then. After one day, I figured it was a good place to stay away from."

Lou sighed. "I wish I had felt the same. I met John King there . . . Will we stay long in Cimarron?"

"No, soon as I can buy a little grub we'll move on. Not knowing where any posse might be, or where King is, we can't take any chances."

"I'll appreciate it if you'll pick me up a couple of sacks of cigarette makings while you're there," Lou said. "What's the next town after Cimarron?"

"Place called Raton; leastwise that's what the marshal said. It'll be another long day's ride."

"Is it still in New Mexico?"

Laverty nodded. "Right close to the Colorado border. I want to cross over soon as we can."

"Don't hold back on my account," Lou said. "I'll keep up with you."

He glanced at the woman and smiled. "Expect you will," he said. "But right now you best get a little sleep—if you can."

"Never tried sleeping in a saddle," Lou said with a smile, "but I guess there's a first time for everything."

"For sure. I got used to it while I was working cattle," Laverty said, watching her tip her hat forward and close her eyes.

He wouldn't mind Henry Pettibone seeing his daughter now. Without the application of cosmetics and the brassy look they gave her, and also without the gaudy, revealing dress she had been wearing when he first saw her in the Castle, she was a young and pretty woman. Tom was sure Henry would have been proud of her.

"What was my pa like?"

Laverty shifted his eyes to her. He'd thought she was asleep, but she had merely closed her eyes.

"He was my good friend. We hit it off together fine."

"Was he real straitlaced? That's the way I remember him."

"Not sure what you mean by that, but if you mean honest and square, he was. Never knew him to beat a man out of anything; fact is, Henry went out of his way to make things right with somebody if there was any call to."

Tom paused, his gaze again on the two riders just topping out a rise to the east. That they, too, were heading for Cimarron was evident. Again the question rose in his mind: Could they be the Morrals? If they were members of a posse, where were the rest of the riders?

"What did my mother die of?"

At Lou's question Tom shook his head. "I don't know. Henry never did say. I didn't know until that day when a steer killed him that he even had a wife—or a daughter."

Tom could have said that Anne Pettibone had probably died of a broken heart after her daughter had run away, but he saw no point to it. Telling Lou that would only serve to deepen the hurt the news of her parents' death had caused.

"I wish I could have seen them just once before it was too late," Lou said. "I always told myself that I would go back someday for a visit—only I never did. Truth is I didn't get a chance."

Lou had closed her eyes once more. Tom noticed that she had been fingering the cameo locket and it now hung motionless against her bosom as her hand sank slowly to her lap. The girl was asleep this time, there was no doubt. Laverty looked ahead. The two riders were still in sight, somewhat closer but not enough to recognize. He had a feeling they were in no way any threat to him and Lou Petty, but were merely pilgrims heading into Cimarron for one purpose or another.

Abruptly Laverty drew to a halt, reaching out to grasp the bridle of Lou's sorrel mare and bring her to a stop also. Voices coming from beyond a clump of brush had reached him.

"What—"

Tom silenced the woman's question before she could complete it.

"Somebody up ahead," he whispered.

Dropping from the saddle, Laverty crossed silently to the stand of rabbit brush and Apache plume growing on the lips of a low bluff. Hunched low, and suddenly aware that Lou was beside him, he cautioned her with a finger to his lips and worked his way to the shrubs. Removing his hat, he stretched out on his belly and, perfectly flat, peered over the edge of the bluff.

A low curse escaped his tightly drawn mouth. It was Ben and Charlie Morral.

19

SURE lucky you knew about that trail through the Turkeys," Charlie Morral was saying. "Put us way ahead of that posse. Where you reckon King is?"

Tom glanced at Lou. "Turkeys?" he whispered.

"The mountains near Pardo. The river runs along the west side of them, the trail's on the east," Lou replied in an equally low voice.

Pulling themselves forward to where they could again look down upon the two men who had apparently halted to rest their horses, Laverty and Lou strained to hear their words.

"I reckon he's somewhere on the river," Ben said with an indifferent wave of his hand. "Wanted to go that way. Figured he knew better 'n me."

"Expect we're way ahead of Gilmore and that posse, too. They wasn't aiming to get started until first light. How much farther've we got to go till we get to Cimarron?"

Ben Morral, taking a pint bottle of whiskey from his pocket, helped himself to a brief swallow. Wiping his mouth with the back of his hand, he passed the liquor on to his brother.

"Ain't far. It's right over there on the yonder side of them little hills."

Charlie had his drink, returned the bottle to Ben. "I'm wondering where that killer is by now."

Morral stared off into the direction of the Sangre de Cristos and the country south where the river would be. "He's somewhere close for damn sure. Expect he's been riding hard, but my guess is we're in front of him."

"What if he don't go to Cimarron, cuts off to one of them other towns?"

"Then we'll light out for Raton. Only way he can go."

"Unless he fooled us and headed east."

"And he could've gone straight up or maybe dug hisself a hole and crawled in it!" Ben said angrily. "He's going to Cheyenne, and the best way's through Raton Pass."

"Was just thinking he might cross us up," Charlie said apologetically.

Ben lay back on an elbow and shook his head. Taking another swallow from the bottle, he stored the container away inside his black-and-white-checked shirt. In the bright sunlight, his red beard and mustache took on a fiery glint and his round face had almost a childlike quality.

"Ain't likely. He'll make a beeline for the pass and figure he's safe once he's across into Colorado."

Charlie, squatted on his haunches, began to roll himself a cigarette. Nearby, their horses were picking at the grass, jerking large chunks of it from the loose soil. There had been a recent rain and the prairie was soft.

"You reckon he's got that gal with him—King's gal?"

Ben shrugged. "Naw, he'd be a fool if he did. Anyway he was in too much of a hurry to let her tag along. Way King talked, she would've left ahead of him."

"That King is sure all fired up about her leaving. Once he catches her she'll sure think twice before she tries it again."

"Can't say I blame King. That Lou was sure the best piece he had around."

Ben glanced up as he was speaking. The sky was a bright blue and clear, and devoid even of the big, broad-winged vultures that could usually be seen soaring lazily about as they searched for prey on the land below. Lowering his gaze, Ben turned his colorless eyes to the south where the trail lay.

"Glad we got the jump on Gilmore and his bunch. That Laverty is my meat. The town can string up old Zack Fish. That'll make the Army happy."

Tom frowned and drew back. What did Ben Morral mean by that? Why would Town Marshal Fish be in danger of being hanged?

"Was a fool thing he done, making that killer a deputy and giving him back his gun," Charlie said, puffing on his cigarette.

"Leaving the cell door unlocked so's Laverty could make a run for it after he cold-cocked that soldier wasn't smart either. Hard to figure what Zack was thinking about. Might've known the town—and the Army—would take it out on him for letting the killer go."

"Expect he's getting too old for the job. He ain't thinking right no more."

Ben laughed. "He won't have to do no worrying about that much longer. That colonel out at the fort wants blood and the town'll have to give it to him to save their own hides. I feel a mite sorry for old Zack. He always kept out of my way."

"I always figured him for plain lazy, so lazy he wouldn't holler sooey if the hogs was eating him,"

Charlie said. "Sure kind of funny why he'd all of a sudden throw in with a killer like Laverty."

"Yeh," Ben said, shrugging his thick shoulders, "but he was the one that done the choosing, and it sure ain't no skin off my nose. This here Laverty's mine. Like I said, them counter jumpers in town and that colonel will have to be satisfied with taking it out on old Zack . . . Let's get going. I want to be in that town before Laverty shows up."

Tom watched as the two men drew themselves up and crossed to their horses, then took up the trailing reins and swung up into their saddles.

He remained silent as the pair struck off in the general direction of Cimarron, evidently, but a short distance to the east. When they were gone from sight, he got to his feet and, reaching down, took Lou Petty by the hand and assisted her to rise.

"Reckon I'll be leaving you here," he said, staring off to the south.

The woman frowned, anxiety in her eyes as she stared at him. "Why?"

"I'm going back to Pardo. You'd best keep on heading north for Cheyenne."

"Pardo! You're going back? Why in heaven's name would you do that; don't you realize you'll be riding straight into a lynching? You heard what the Morrals said."

"Sure did."

"You go there and they'll hang both you and the marshal."

"Maybe not. One thing sure, I can't let them hang Zack for what he done for me," Laverty said as they moved slowly off the bluff.

"So to fix that you aim to let them hang you both!"

Laverty grinned. "Not exactly—not if I can help it."

"What chance will you have? The whole town and the Army will be keeping an eye on the marshal. You won't be able to even get close to him if you're figuring to break him out of jail. You'll just be putting a noose around your neck for nothing!"

"Aim to do my moving around at night. In the dark maybe nobody'll spot me and—"

"Being dark doesn't mean a thing in Pardo! People are out and around same as if it were daylight."

"I got by last night without being seen," Laverty said. "Anyway I have to take the chance. I see now Zack Fish was my friend, and I sure don't figure to let him down . . . Now, best thing for you to do is pass up Cimarron and just keep going till you come to Raton. I'll give you what grub I've got so's you can make out—"

"I have some food," Lou cut in dully.

"When you get to Raton the next thing to do is cross over into Colorado. Sure wouldn't waste much time doing that. If King's still chasing you, head for a town called Trinidad. The lawman there's named Henline. He's a friend of Zack's. Tell him about King and ask him to help you."

They reached the horses, contentedly grazing on the sweet grass that covered the land.

147

"Your mare's in good shape," Tom said, eyeing the sorrel critically. "Don't be afraid to push her hard. The sooner you're in Colorado the better off you'll be."

Lou Petty hesitated, one hand holding the mare's reins, the other grasping the saddle horn as she prepared to mount.

"Then you're dead set on going back to Pardo?"

"No choice," Laverty replied, helping the woman onto her horse and then climbing onto his own. "Zack needs my help. I aim to give it to him, same as he helped me . . . Good luck—and stay out of sight much as you can."

Lou Petty shook her head. "Save your advice; I'm not riding on. I'm going back with you."

"The hell you are! I can't let you—"

"I can do what I please; you told me that yourself," Lou snapped. "It's my choice."

"Maybe, but it sure ain't smart."

"The way I see it, it is. Comes down to this: I know the town pretty good and I can help you get around without being seen." She paused, faced him squarely. "Besides I've got a personal stake in this. It comes to me all of a sudden that there wasn't any use of me going anywhere without you."

Laverty rubbed at his jaw, his forehead furrowed. "Don't figure that's smart either. Not much future in lining up with me—and I'm not all that sure I want a partner."

A stricken look crossed Lou's face. "I was hoping that maybe you—me—" she began, and then allowed her voice to trail off into nothing. Abruptly she straightened in her saddle. "Makes no difference; I'm not going on alone. Which way do we take back to Pardo, the trail or the road by the river?"

Laverty considered her for a long breath and smiled. "Shortest way's through the Turkey Mountains going by what the Morrals said, but I don't know the trail and I'd sure hate to get lost. I reckon maybe we ought to—"

A strange look on Lou's face caused Laverty to hush. Her eyes widened in fear and her lips became a straight line as she stared at something beyond him.

"Tom," she murmured in a lost voice.

Realization came swiftly to Laverty. His hand dropped to the gun on his hip. In that same instant of time the voice of John King reached him.

"Don't try it, mister! I could put a bullet in your head easy but I've got to save you for Ben Morral. Raise your hands!"

20

CURSING his own carelessness, Tom raised his hands slowly and turned around. He should have kept a better watch on his back trail, but as he and Lou drew nearer to the settlement of Cimarron, he had grown overconfident.

With King was Jess Farley, the friend of Kurt Morral. He was astride a tall chestnut while King was on a black, white-stockinged gelding. Both men had their guns out, were keeping them leveled on Laverty.

Tom cast a side glance at Lou Petty, a feeling of guilt and of failing her sweeping through him. Her face was taut and fear still filled her eyes, but she said nothing as the two men rode toward them from the low brushy hill behind which they had halted. No doubt they had spotted Lou and him some distance away and had worked their way in quietly, using the hill as cover.

"Figured we were about to catch up to you," King said, his face immobile. "Obliged to you for looking out for my woman, but I expect she slowed you down some."

"Can bet she sure did," Farley said slyly.

Laverty stiffened with anger and cursed himself again for not keeping a better watch on their trail. King swung his horse to the side and rode in close to Lou. His dark eyes glittered and his lips were set in a hard, straight line.

"You know better than to try leaving me," he snarled, and, quick as a rattlesnake, raised his hand and struck the woman a blow across the side of her head.

As Lou reeled in her saddle Laverty, ignoring Farley, threw himself off the bay at King. As they came together King went off his horse, and together they struck the ground with a solid impact.

"Don't you ever hit her again!" Laverty yelled, grasping the saloon man by the collar of his coat and driving a rock-hard fist into the man's jaw.

In the next moment the unforgiving bone and metal

butt of Jess Farley's six-gun smashed into the side of Tom's head. A burst of lights filled his eyes and then blackness claimed him.

Laverty returned to consciousness slowly. Farley was standing over him, a sardonic grin on his angular face. He had brushed his high-crowned hat to the back of his skull and was sucking on a limp brown-paper cigarette.

Tom, still dazed as pain throbbed through him in sickening waves, focused his eyes and glanced to the side where he had last seen Lou and John King. They were again in the saddle and were looking down at him, the girl with apprehension, King with a sullen sort of satisfaction.

"You want to try that again, drifter?" Farley asked in a derisive tone. "Expect that head of yours'll bust before my gun will."

Tom pulled himself to his feet, attention on the woman. Apparently King had struck her several more times, as her face was flushed and beginning to discolor in several places.

"Get on your horse," Farley ordered. "Ben's waiting for you at Cimarron by now, I expect."

Laverty turned to the bay, feeling the lightness of an empty holster on his hip, and swung up into the saddle. He had fixed things up good for both Lou and himself, he thought, and it looked as if there was no way out. The girl was back in the hands of John King, and the two Morral brothers were waiting in Cimarron to kill him. Raising his eyes, he glanced at Lou. She was now looking at him from beneath the brim of her hat, a faint smile on her bruised lips. Instantly a gust of raw anger surged through Laverty, but before he could move he felt the hard, round muzzle of Farley's gun jab into his spine.

"Forget it," Farley said quietly. "Point for them bluffs on ahead, and if you make one wrong move I'll blow you off that horse. Ben wants you for himself, but he wouldn't fault me none if I had to shoot you trying to get away."

Tom swung the bay around in the direction indicated. His glance caught that of John King.

"I'll kill you for what you've done to her!" he said in a low, grinding voice.

King laughed. "Doubt that, cowboy. In another hour you'll be a dead man."

"Not dead yet," Laverty said, "so don't—"

"Move on, move on!" Farley cut in, gesturing impatiently. "Ben's awaiting!"

Laverty started the bay up the slight incline that lay before them. Farley, gun out and ready, veered in directly behind him. Following the saloon man and riding side by side were Lou Petty and King.

An hour later they broke out of some low hills and saw Cimarron, a small scatter of buildings immediately ahead. There appeared to be little to the town at first glance, but as they drew nearer Tom saw that it offered an inn, two general stores, a like number of saloons, a livery stable, and four or five other business concerns.

"There's Ben," Farley said. "Head over to him."

Laverty had caught sight of Morral and his brother in the same moment. They were standing in the shade of a building, one of the general stores at the near end of the settlement. His mind racing to find a way to meet and overcome the danger that faced him, Tom rode slowly toward the two men.

"I see you got them both," Ben Morral said as they drew up before him and Charlie. "All right, get the killer off that horse. Want to settle with him before Gilmore and his bunch gets here."

Laverty, tension mounting but outwardly cool, climbed down from the bay without any prompting from Farley. He wasn't sure what to expect; did Ben Morral intend to stand him up against the side of the nearby building and shoot him? If so there was little he could do other than to make a break for it, try to reach Morral and overpower him before he could use his weapon—and the odds for him being successful in doing that were overwhelmingly against him.

Given a gun and confronting the man in a fair shoot-out, Tom felt he would have a good chance of seeing the next sunrise. Not a gunman in the full sense of the word, he nevertheless was no stranger to a six-gun, having taught himself to use a weapon fast and accurately, thanks to the long, lonely hours on the range when the cattle were grazing and he could ride off a reasonable distance and practice.

Having nothing else to do with his monthly wages other than have a good time in one of the saloons that flourished in the San Pedro River country, he had kept himself well supplied with ammunition that he never hesitated to use on whatever targets—cans, bottles, cactus buds, and the like—that were around.

Kurt Morral was the first man he had killed, and Tom had been sickened by the act. But he had consoled himself with the knowledge that he'd had no choice but to draw and shoot fast or get shot himself.

"So you're the saddlebum that killed Kurt?" Ben said as Tom faced him.

Morral's broad features were flushed and his deep-set eyes appeared to be of granite. He wore his gun well forward on his right leg, Laverty noted. Charlie carried no pistol, had instead a long, sheathed hunting knife hanging from his belt.

"Was him that made the first move," Tom said in a level voice.

The storekeeper had come out of his building and joined several other men standing on the landing and looking on with interest. Farther down the wide, irregular street, two other residents of Cimarron were hurrying up.

Tom threw a quick glance at Lou Petty, still mounted and with King close by. Her eyes looked soft and were filled with care. King intended to keep her there, force her to witness the execution, that was plain.

"That's what you say!" Charlie Morral said, shaking his head. "It ain't how we heard it."

"If you heard it any other way, you heard a lie,"

Laverty said coldly. "I—"

"Don't make a goddamn bit of difference to me how it happened!" Ben said, his voice rising. "You killed my brother, now you'll answer to me. Give him back his gun, Jess."

Farley frowned, hesitated. "You for sure you—"

"You heard me!" Ben snarled. "We'll just see if this bastard's as handy with an iron against a sober man as he was a drunk."

Farley shrugged and, not moving, tossed Tom his weapon. Laverty caught it by the butt, a feeling of confidence and reassurance sweeping away the misgivings that filled him. Thumbing the catch, he spun the cylinder, making certain it was free and fully loaded, and then, snapping it back in place, he slid the heavy .45 back into the holster.

A coolness like an early morning breeze had come over him. He was on equal terms with Ben Morral now—thanks to the man's towering arrogance—and was ready to take his chances in a stand-up shoot-out. Turning slightly, he smiled at Lou Petty and then shifted his attention to Ben Morral.

"This between just you and me or am I taking on your brother and Farley, too?"

"Don't figure it'll matter to you once this is over," Morral said, spreading his legs and settling himself squarely in the loose dust. "Make your move."

"Leaving that up to you. I don't want to shoot you any more than I did Kurt."

Morral grinned, a broad, toothy grimace that displayed his hatred for the man who had slain his brother.

"Have it your way then, goddamm you!" he yelled, and made a stab for his gun.

Laverty reacted instantly. His hand swept down, came up with the .45 glinting dully in the sunlight. He raised, cocked, and triggered the weapon in a single, fluid motion. Ben fired also but the echoing report came a heartbeat after Tom's gun. He staggered back, fell against the side of the building, and sank to the ground.

All the hours of aimless practice designed for nothing more than to pass the time had paid off for Tom Laverty, and as smoke billowed up around him and the echoes continued to roll, he pivoted to face Farley.

Morral's friend threw up both hands and took a hasty step backward. "Not me!" he said. "This ain't my fight!"

"Look out!" one of the men on the store landing shouted.

Tom instinctively rocked to one side and wheeled. Charlie Morral, face livid with fury, red hair shining in the sunlight, and huge arms extended, was charging straight for him.

"You killed Kurt, now you've gone and killed Ben!" he shouted. "I ain't letting you get away with it!"

In the following instant Tom felt the solid impact of Charlie Morral crashing into him. Gun flying from his hand, he fought to keep his footing, but to no avail.

With Charlie's huge fists hammering on him, and the burly man's weight carrying him off balance, he went down into the dust.

21

L AVERTY'S breath exploded from his flaring mouth in a gusty blast as Morral's weight came down upon him. Jerking his head to one side, he avoided Charlie's fists and, freeing one leg, brought it up hard into the man's groin. Charlie, crouched over Laverty, cursed and pulled back. Instantly Tom kicked free and, falling to one side, bounded to his feet in the boiling cloud of dust the scuffle had lifted.

Whirling, Tom met Charlie Morral, also on his feet and coming at him again. Dodging to one side, Laverty avoided a wild right swing by Morral and, as the big man stumbled by, drove his fist into his jaw.

Morral, barely fazed, shook his head, spun, and came charging back. Once more Tom avoided the man's sledging fists and sent a left and then a right smashing into Charlie's head. Morral bellowed, came around again. Muscular arms bared to the shoulders and extended as before to encompass Laverty, he closed in. Laverty was fully aware that he must avoid the burly Morral; being trapped in the powerful grasp of Charlie Morral would be the equivalent of being hugged by a grizzly, and no doubt just as fatal.

Dancing away, he dodged the sweaty, heaving, dust-plastered man, keeping well clear of him until he was able to move in fast, drive two more sharp blows to Charlie's jaw, and pull back. He continued this for several minutes, hearing encouragement from several of the bystanders.

"Damn you, stand still!" Morral yelled, coming to a flat-footed halt.

Laverty, breathing heavily, arms heavy as lead, paused also. "Can call it off if you're willing. This won't prove anything."

"You killed my brothers!" Charlie yelled, and lunged. "I'm going to make you pay for that!"

Tom, expecting the move, put all his flagging strength into a right to Morral's jaw and a stiff left into the man's belly as he plunged forward. Morral grunted and, for the first time, seemed hurt by Laverty's fists.

Quick to seize the opportunity, Tom rushed in, hammering rights and lefts to the husky man's jaw and body. Morral, head wobbling under the attack, began to sink to the ground. On his knees he rocked forward, braced himself with his arms, big hands all but buried in the loose dust.

Laverty, merciless, did not hold back but continued the attack. Arms growing heavier with each fleeting moment, he knew his blows carried little power now, but he had to knock Charlie Morral out or the fight would continue.

Suddenly he felt Morral's arms wrap about his legs. He had gotten in too close and Charlie had grabbed him. Locking his hands together, Tom began to rain blows on the man's head and thick shoulders. Morral seemed unmindful and tightened his grip around Laverty's legs.

Abruptly Tom toppled to the ground. Morral, slightly dazed and slow to react, fell forward upon him, a knife now in his hand. As sunlight glittered off the razor-sharp Green River, Laverty desperately struggled to jerk away, but only partly succeeded.

He saw the flash of the blade as it descended. It missed his throat by only an inch. Continuing to move, Tom squirmed away as Morral slashed at him again.

"Here!" he heard a voice yell.

His gun made a thudding sound as it fell to the ground beside him. Someone in the crowd, not liking the uneven turn the fight had taken, had retrieved his weapon and tossed it to him. Seizing the .45, Laverty, flat on his back, leveled the weapon at Morral.

"Back off," he shouted, "or I'll shoot."

"The hell you will!" Charlie yelled in a wild voice, and rising to his knees, long blade poised, threw himself at Laverty.

Tom fired, hearing the grate of sand in the weapon's mechanism as he did. He took no aim, simply triggered the gun in hopes of stopping the vengeance-crazed Charlie. It did—but briefly. The bullet struck Morral in the fleshy part of his right leg. On his knees, supporting himself by one hand on the ground, the other clutching the knife upraised and ready to strike, he lurched forward.

"I ain't done yet!" he yelled.

Tom threw himself to one side; there was no time to get to his feet. He triggered his gun once more—again in haste, firing blindly. Through the smoke and dust haze he saw Morral jolt, stagger to one side. Charlie hung there for what seemed an interminably long time, his broad, coarse face covered with dirt and litter from the street, mouth agape, blazing eyes dulling slowly. And then, without uttering a sound, he collapsed.

Laverty drew himself upright slowly. He was aching from the blows he had taken from Morral's powerful fists and was still sucking deep for breath. Wiping the dust and sand from his weapon, he rodded out the spent cartridges and refilled the cylinder from the supply in his belt. Nearby the crowd of bystanders had moved in closer, some pausing to bend over Charlie Morral, others slapping Tom on the back and expressing their congratulations.

"This one ain't dead—only bad hurt," one of those looking down at Charlie said. "Couple of you give me a hand, help me get him over to Doc Williams."

"There ain't no point carrying the other 'n over to his place," a different voice said. "He's deader'n a doornail."

Tom heard only vaguely. Breathing easier, he turned his glance to where he had last seen Lou Petty and John King. They were not there. Nor was there any sign of Jess Farley. He turned to a man close by.

"The woman and the man that were here. Did you

see where they went?"

"Them two—the woman on the sorrel and him on a black—they left awhile back. It was when you and the big fellow was going at it tooth and nail," the man answered, his ruddy features wreathed in a smile at the personal honor of being singled out by Laverty for conversation. "Other fellow went with them too . . . Sure like to say that was one hell of a fight! I sure figured you was a goner when he come up with that big toad-stabber."

Tom nodded, smiled tightly. "Was a close one, all right. Owe whoever tossed my gun to me a big favor . . . You see which way the woman and the men went when they rode out?"

"Yeh, they all headed south down the trail. Seemed in a real big hurry."

Laverty said, "Obliged," and looked off in the direction Lou and the men had taken. They would be heading back to Pardo.

"How long ago did you say it was when they left?"

"Ten, maybe fifteen minutes."

With no greater lead than that, he would stand a good chance of overtaking them, Tom thought. Their horses were in no better condition than his own.

"Like to ask a favor: you mind looking after my packhorse?" he said then, turning to the ruddy-faced bystander.

"I'll be glad to see to him," the man replied. "I'll put him in Slim Johnson's stable.

"I'll appreciate that. Can tell Johnson I'll be back in

a couple of days for him," Tom said, and started toward the hitch rack at the side of the store where someone had tied the bay.

Four men were carrying Charlie Morral off down the street while three others had taken Ben's body and were heading for the building over the door of which was the black and white sign: UNDERTAKER.

If he rode out immediately and pushed the gelding hard, he should be able to catch up with Lou and the two men before they got too far down the trail, he assured himself again. It was still hours until dark, and he should be able to spot them ahead.

"Got some talking to do to you," a deep voice said from nearby. "Just you hold up a bit. What's your name?"

Tom halted, turned to see who had spoken. A young man about his age, wearing ordinary range clothing but with a deputy sheriff's star pinned to the pocket of his shirt, was considering him coldly.

"Laverty," Tom said.

Arms folded across his chest, the deputy continued to stare. "From where?"

"Arizona—the San Pedro River country."

"Well, I don't know how it is down there but up here we don't take kindly to strangers blowing in and killing—"

"Hell, McGreavy, you got no call to jail this man!" the ruddy-faced bystander declared, stepping up to Laverty's side. "Was a fair fight. There's two dozen that seen it and will tell you so."

"Maybe it was," the deputy said, "but you know how the sheriff feels about shootings in town. He's been touchy as all getout ever since Clay Allison got to hanging around."

"But this here was a fair fight—a shoot-out! Dead man went for his gun first, but this fellow here, he was a mite faster."

Two other men from the dissipating crowd paused nearby. One, a tall, well-dressed individual who looked to be a prosperous rancher, nodded.

"Pete's right, Mac. And not only that, after he'd shot it out fair and square with one of them, the brother, somebody said he was, jumped him and started a fight. When he started getting the worst of it, he went for his knife. Man couldn't do anything but protect himself."

"And that one ain't dead. Morrison said he'd be all right. Just won't move around as fast as he'd maybe like to."

McGreavy nodded patiently. "I'm hearing what you're all saying and I ain't denying any of it. Seen the last part myself. But I've got my duty—and you know how the sheriff is. He wants a written report on anything like this . . . Come on, Laverty, this won't take long."

Tom swore softly as the deputy gestured toward the building housing the lawman's office and jail. A delay would cost him time that would have enabled him to overtake King and the others.

"I don't want no trouble with you," McGreavy said,

deftly pulling Tom's gun from its holster. "Let's go. Like I said, this will take only a few minutes."

22

DEPUTY SHERIFF McGREAVY'S few minutes proved to be slightly more than an hour.

As he came out of the lawman's office Tom glanced at the sun. It was not yet noon, but he could forget about catching up with Lou and the two men; in fact, he would have to press his horse to reach Pardo by midnight.

"You'll find that bay of yours down at the livery," McGreavy said from the doorway. "Pete Goodman took him there along with your packhorse."

Laverty nodded, glanced down the street to the broad, tin-roofed building that was the stable. Wordless, irritated, he turned away and struck off through the dust.

"Can oblige me by staying out of my town," McGreavy called after him. "We got enough trouble up here without you bringing in yours."

Laverty shrugged and continued on toward the livery barn. "None of it was my choosing," he said, more to himself than to the deputy.

The man called Pete was standing in the runway of the stable talking to a tall, sharp-nosed man in overalls—either the owner or a hostler—as he entered.

"Here he is now," Pete said importantly. "Mr. Laverty wants you to look after his packhorse while he's gone. This here's Slim Johnson, Mr. Laverty. He owns the stable."

Tom took Johnson's hand into his own at the introduction. "Guess Pete told you it'd be for only a couple of days. Can leave the bay, too, if you've got a good horse I can ride. He's had it pretty hard for the last couple of days."

Johnson glanced at the bay standing in a nearby stall. The place had a rank odor as if it had not been cleaned out in weeks—which could account for the lack of patrons.

"Like to accommodate you," Johnson said, "but truth is I ain't got a thing fit for a man to ride. How long did you say you'd be gone?"

"Two, maybe three days; it's hard to say. You want your pay in advance?"

Johnson shook his head. "Didn't mean it that way. It won't be needful; the buckskin'll stand good for the feed bill. You want anything off that pack saddle?"

"No," Laverty replied as he crossed to the bay and climbed up into the saddle. "I'm in a hurry and won't be stopping to eat. You figure the fastest way to Fort Union is down the trail?"

"Sure is," Pete said promptly. "Maybe a mite longer 'n the road along the river, but it's better and a horse can travel a lot faster."

"Where do I get on it?"

"Take the road south out of town till you come to the forks, then turn right; that'll be about twenty mile from here. Could maybe save a little time cutting across country and hit the trail about twenty-five miles below here."

"Be a lot rougher going," Pete said. "You get some hogbacks off the mountains straggling out there onto the flats. Real hard on a horse."

"Reckon I'll stick to the trail," Tom said, and nodding his thanks to the men, rode out into the bright, warm sunshine, and turned south.

Taking the trail would save time, Laverty thought. While the bay was a big, strong horse, he had not had much rest, and rough country would rob him of his strength. Tom glanced up at the sun. With luck, he should reach Pardo by midnight, a good time for him to be riding into the settlement.

He wished he could get there sooner for Lou Petty's sake. There was nothing he could do at the moment to prevent John King from venting his rage upon the girl; he could only hope that King would wait until he arrived in Pardo before punishing her. He had warned the saloon man to never lay a hand on her again, but such would carry little weight with King. With his great sense of self-importance, John King would accept a warning from no one. Too, he no doubt considered Tom Laverty dead; even though he had watched Ben Morral die, he would have reassured himself by the belief that Charlie would get the job done.

When it came to Zack Fish, he had no idea what he would be up against in Pardo. It could be the Army had taken charge of the old lawman and soldiers now stood guard over him. It wouldn't matter; civilian or soldiers, he'd get Zack out of jail somehow—by trickery or bullets, whichever was necessary. And considering the lateness of the hour when he would be making the attempt, and the fact that the area around the jail was usually deserted at that time, he shouldn't find the task too difficult.

A little over an hour later he was on the trail and bearing steadily south. He passed several canvas-topped wagons heading in the same direction, the passengers of which all waved and sang out a greeting as if happy to see him. He responded in kind but did not stop.

Around two o'clock, however, he did pull well off the road and put his attention on a group of riders who had halted beside a spur of trees thrusting out from the nearby hills. Tom remained in the brush and other scrubby growth flanking the trail at a distance until he had reached a point directly behind the party, several members of which appeared familiar.

Dismounting, he tied the gelding to a stumpy juniper from which a jay scolded him noisily for disturbing his feeding on the small, blue berries, and made his way forward through the brush to where he could get a better look at the riders.

He had been right. It was Nate Gilmore and a posse that contained several men he'd seen the night before in front of the jail. They were all hunched about a low fire over which a pot of coffee had been put to boil, talking and smoking while they waited.

"Ain't no big hurry," Laverty heard Gilmore say. The proprietor of the Paris Saloon was squatting, back to a stump, puffing on a cigar. "That drifter's dead by now. He might've gunned down Ben somehow, but he's got about as much chance of getting away from Charlie and that big knife of his as I have of kissing the queen of Spain."

Evidently King and Lou had met Gilmore in their passage south and had stopped to talk. That was encouraging to Laverty; they would not be as far ahead now as he'd feared.

"You ain't said why we have to keep going to Cimarron," one of the posse members said. "Why can't we just turn around and head back for town?"

"Got to have the body," Gilmore replied. "Figured you all would know that. Need to show the colonel that the killer is dead. Only way we're going to get the Army off our backs."

"Hell, just tell him—"

"Colonels ain't ones to take a man's word for anything, specially in something like this. They've got to see it with their own eyes."

"Seems to me having Zack Fish all locked up and waiting to get hung ought to be enough for the Army."

"You're forgetting Zack didn't kill anybody. He just fixed it so's the killer could get away. That makes him almost as guilty as this Laverty, but not as much. I figure giving them both to the colonel will patch things up good for us."

"Till somebody else shoots somebody," a man said

dryly, reaching for the coffeepot. "Then it'll start all over again."

"That ain't going to happen. I talked things over with King and Hazlett and some of the others. We're going to make it a law that a man can't carry a gun while he's in town, and we're going to hire on a marshal that'll be tough enough to enforce it. Expect we'll have to go to Dodge or maybe Wichita to find the man we want, but we'll get him."

He'd wasted enough time and the bay would have rested a bit, Tom decided, and dropped back quietly to where he had left the horse. He'd learned a couple of things that were important to him, one being that he need not fear any trouble from Gilmore and his posse; they were continuing on to Cimarron. And Zack was still all right. Mounting up, Laverty resumed the ride south a half mile or so and then cut back to the trail, certain he could not be seen by Nate or any of his followers.

Near dark, Tom halted by a small stream to again rest the bay. He'd seen no signs of Lou Petty and King, reckoned they were much farther ahead than he'd hoped. He could use some coffee and a bite to eat but his stock of provisions, although low, was on the packhorse back in Cimarron.

His last meal had been back near Rayado where he had run into Lou. She had been waiting for him, she'd said, and that had disturbed him. Tom hoped the woman was not counting too strongly on him. Once he got Zack Fish out of jail and safely on his way—

and that obligation fulfilled—and Lou was rid of John King, he'd be on his way again. Settling down to a marriage was the last thing he had in mind.

Somewhere in the vicinity of Ocate Crossing, Tom abandoned the trail and angled cross-country toward where he figured Pardo would be. By so doing he would be above the fort and less likely to encounter any army patrols that for some reason might be out.

Gaining the trail along the Mora River, he continued south. The bay was now moving at a slow, tired walk, unable to maintain any longer the steady lope he'd held almost since leaving Cimarron. Laverty, too, was feeling the drag of the hours. Slumped in the saddle, shoulders pitched forward, head down, he had his eyes closed but he was not sleeping. He was simply following the custom of all men who spend much time on a horse, dozing occasionally but never fully asleep.

He heard Pardo before it even came into sight. Sounds carrying through the cool night reached him as he broke out of the low hills onto the flats. A short time later, the glow of light from the saloons and those along the street, as well as others in the business houses still open and greedy for business, threw a faint, yellow halo over the settlement.

Laverty heaved a sigh of relief as he straightened up in his saddle. He was back at last; all he had to do now was find Lou Petty, break Zack Fish out of jail, and leave Pardo without being caught.

23

TOM LAVERTY kept to the long shadows after he left the protection of the brush and trees along the river, and entered the town proper along the rear of a dark, abandoned building—once a feed and grain store, he guessed from the looks of it.

There were a number of men, both soldiers and civilians, on the street, and all of the saloons appeared to be operating full blast with loud talking, singing, laughter, and piano and string instrument music issuing from their open doors. There was a bright moon, and its light combined with that of the lamps turned the active settlement almost into day.

Tom guided the weary bay to the rear of King's Castle and halted there, undecided whether to risk entering the noisy, and no doubt well-attended, saloon in search of Lou or not. Gilmore and his posse would not be around, he knew, but there would be those who would recognize him and that could only mean trouble.

At that moment one of the women, accompanied by a soldier, came out the back door of the Castle and headed for the small huts at its rear. Keeping his hat tipped down to hide his features, Tom kneed the bay toward them.

"Did you see Lou Petty in there?" he asked, jerking a thumb at the saloon.

"She ain't working tonight," the woman replied with

a shake of her head.

"Know where I can find her?"

The soldier with the woman yanked impatiently at her arm. "Come on, let's get going."

The woman pointed to one of the shacks. "Expect you'll find her in there, but she ain't—"

Her words broke off abruptly as the soldier, unwilling to delay longer, jerked her half about and sent her stumbling toward the row of shacks.

Tom, wheeling the bay about, pulled up to a hitching post near the first shack and, dismounting, tied the gelding to it. Dropping his hand to the gun on his hip to make certain of its presence, he moved it forward to a more convenient position and then walked quickly to the hut the woman had indicated. Lamplight showed in the heavily curtained window, and stepping up onto the small landing, Tom raised a hand to knock. He paused. The unmistakable sound of flesh meeting flesh violently as someone was slapped, of a cry, and of sobbing came to him. Anger rushed through Laverty. He was in luck; he'd found Lou—and John King. Hesitating no longer, Laverty lifted his leg and booted the door open.

The anger within him soared to fury. Lying on the floor was Lou. Standing astride her, one hand grasping the girl by an arm, the other raised to deliver another blow, was King.

"You!" the saloon man gasped, surprise flooding his features. "I'll—" he added, and reaching inside his coat for the weapon he carried there, spun to face Laverty.

Tom, kicking the door closed to prevent any interference, was upon him before he could draw the revolver. Seizing King by the front of his coat, Tom swung the man about and slammed him up against the wall. As Lou scrambled to her feet Laverty drove a solid blow into King's belly and, as the man buckled forward, dropping the gun, smashed a fist into his jaw.

"No, don't," King moaned, eyes rolling wildly.

Sucking for wind, Tom, stepped back, fist cocked for another shocking blow to King's head, as the man sank slowly to the floor. Laverty threw a glance at the woman. She was still wearing the clothing she'd had on when they'd met on the trail, an indication that she and King had reached Pardo only a short time before him.

"Get ready to travel," he snapped, and relaxing his fist, reached down and, again taking King by the front of his coat, dragged him to his feet and shoved him onto the bed.

"No, no more," the saloon man muttered.

Ignoring the half-conscious King's pleas, Tom jerked one of the worn blankets from the bed and ripped it into several strips. Bending over King, he tied the man's hands behind his back, bound his feet together, and then with a third strip of the cloth, lashed all four members into one as a man might bind a deer for a pole portage.

Turning about Tom faced Lou. "Told him I'd kill him if he beat you again. Still can if it's what you want."

Lou shook her head. "There's been too much killing." She had her wool jacket and narrow-brimmed hat on again and was ready to ride, and despite her bruised face and lips and discolored eyes, she smiled. "Anyway he's not worth it."

Laverty shrugged and moved to the door. "Think you're able to do some more riding?" he asked, opening the flimsy panel and looking about. There was no one in sight. "Might be best if you'd go some-where and rest a bit—at some friend's place maybe."

"I've got no friends I can trust," Lou said flatly. "Anyway, I'll be all right. I'd rather you'd throw me across a saddle like a sack of grain and get me out of here than leave me."

"Then let's go," Laverty said, and stepped out into the open.

Lou followed woodenly. Weariness dragged at her battered features and her eyes were all but closed, but she uttered no complaint.

"Where's your horse?" Laverty asked.

"Out back."

"We'll get her, then go by the jail. Next thing is to get Zack out of that cell."

Lou made no comment and together they left the shack, gathering the two horses, and keeping to the back of the buildings, made their way to the jail. A horse stood in the shed to the rear of the structure where Tom, that previous night, had half expected Zack Fish to bring his animals.

"What happened in Cimarron after we left?" Lou

asked in a low voice as they secured their mounts to a nearby tree. "I was there when you killed Ben, but what about Charlie? We rode off just when he ran at you and knocked you down. King was sure he'd kill you."

"Tried hard enough," Laverty replied. "Had to shoot him too—twice—but somebody said he'd live."

"You should have killed him. He was no better than Kurt or Ben."

"Thought I heard you say there'd been too much killing."

Lou sighed and shook her head. "Oh, I don't know what to think! I only know I'll be glad to get as far away as I can from Pardo . . . Won't they have the marshal guarded?" she added as they moved quietly along the side of the building.

Tom nodded. "Bound to."

"Then how—"

"Can answer that when the time comes," Laverty said, halting at the corner of the structure and looking up and down the street. As was usual, all activity was up where the saloons were; there was no one anywhere near the jail.

"Best you wait here," Laverty said quietly. "Don't know for sure what I'm walking into and I don't want you caught in the middle of it." He paused, then said: "If this don't work out and I don't make it back, get your horse and ride on—unless you're of a mind to stay and go back to work with King."

"No, I'll never do that. I'll ride on," Lou said, "but

I'm figuring on you coming back. I'll be here."

Tom grinned. "Just hope you won't be sorry," he said. "Whatever, it won't take long either way."

Again scanning the street closely to be certain that all was clear at that end, he rounded the corner of the building housing the jail and crossed to the door. He frowned, swore under his breath. The thick panel was closed. He had expected to find it open as it usually was and had laid his plans accordingly, but that was out now.

Hesitating only briefly, he reached out and knocked firmly. Chair legs scraped against the floor and then came the grating sound of a lock being turned. The door opened to a narrow crack.

"Who's there?" a voice asked cautiously.

"Me," Laverty said, and threw his weight against the thick panel.

The door thudded against the man standing behind it. Tom had a glimpse of him stumbling backward across the room and crashing into the opposite wall as he hastily stepped inside. Gun out and ready, he swept the dimly lit room with a sharp, probing look. There was no one else; apparently only one guard, a civilian and not a soldier, had been posted to guard Fish.

Crossing to the stunned jailer, Tom pulled him to his feet, and taking the ring of keys from its peg, he moved into the cell area, pushing, half carrying the guard with him.

"What's going on out there?" Zack Fish asked sleepily. "What's all that damned racket?"

Tom pushed the jailer into the empty cell next to the one the old marshal occupied and locked the door.

"Who the hell are you?" Fish continued, and then checked himself abruptly. "Is that you, Tom?"

"It is," Laverty replied as he unlocked Zack's cell door. "I'm a bit late getting here, but I made it. Come on, let's get moving."

Fish came out of the cage hurriedly, pulling on his hat as he did. "I don't savvy none of this! I figured you'd be somewheres on the way to Cheyenne. What are you doing here?"

"Heard they'd locked you up because of what you did for me. Couldn't let them do that . . . Get your gun; you may need it."

Fish crossed to the table, pulled open a drawer, and reclaimed his gun and belt.

"Sure obliged to you, Tom, but you're only making things worse for yourself. The Army's watching the town real close, seeing as how the merchants asked the colonel to give them a hand in cleaning up the place."

"Kind of got that idea from what I've heard. And seems you—and me if they could catch me—were to be the first ones hung as good examples. Speaking of soldiers, I didn't see many when I rode in," Laverty said, watching Zack buckle on his gun belt. "If—"

"Somebody's coming," Lou Petty warned from the doorway.

Laverty crossed quickly to where he could see the street. Cavalrymen. He turned to the older man. "Got to move fast. There's a half-a-dozen soldiers coming. Is that your horse in the shed?"

Fish nodded, glanced at the woman. "Howdy, Lou. Sure pleased to see you again . . . Yeh, that's my horse. Been there since yesterday. Been trying to get somebody to stable him for me but nobody'd bother. Where we going?"

"You know this country better than I do," Laverty said in an urgent voice as they joined Lou in the open. Hurrying, all three crossed to the corner of the building and turned into the shadows.

"Any good place around here close where we can hole up? Our horses have had a long day. Not good for much more traveling."

"That's what's kind of bothering me," Fish said. "When they go to hunting us—and that'll be right soon when them soldiers find Rufus in that cell— they'll figure we ain't gone far. Might be smart to just line out east for Texas, then pull up and hide after we've gone a ways."

They reached the shed. "Might be the thing to do, all right," Laverty said, "but it'll have to be what you and Lou want. I've got to go back to Cimarron. Left my packhorse and gear up there."

"I've been wondering about him," Lou said as they climbed into their saddles. "When you shot Ben—"

"You kill Ben Morral?" Fish asked in an awed voice.

"He gave me no choice."

"And Charlie? What about him? They always run together."

"He's not dead," Tom said. "Shot him up a little but—"

"Help! Somebody help! Here in the jail!"

The voice of the jailer, somewhat muffled, reached out into the night. "Somebody come open up this cell!"

Laverty grinned tightly. "Figured I had him knocked out for a spell," he muttered as they swung away from the shed.

Fish shook his head. "Rufus is a tough old coot. Was probably just playing possum till we got away from the jail."

"There they go!" a voice shouted from the street. "Back of the jail!"

Tom threw a glance over his shoulder. He should have taken time to gag and hog-tie the jailer. Perhaps in so doing he would have bought them a few more minutes' time—although the cavalrymen he'd seen approaching would have found Rufus shortly anyhow.

"You all follow me," Fish said grimly. "There's a cabin a ways below here. I plumb forgot all about it. Maybe we can hole up there till them soldiers get tired of looking for us."

24

THEY rushed on through the night, Lou's mare and Laverty's gelding keeping up with Fish's horse as best they could. The old lawman had chosen to stay in the trees and scrub growth, seeking as much cover from the bright moonlight as possible. It was hard going but doubtless worth the effort.

Back in the street shots could be heard. Zack glanced back over his shoulder. "Got a hunch them yellowlegs and some of the townsfolk are rigging up a posse. Rufus must've recognized you, Tom."

"Expect he did," Laverty said, raising his voice to be heard above the horses. "Was face-to-face there in the doorway for a few seconds. How much farther?"

"Cabin's right on ahead a mile or so. I don't figure anybody'll recollect it. Hardly anybody ever comes this way."

Tom glanced at Lou. She was leaning forward in her saddle, both hands gripping the horn. In the occasional shafts of moonlight streaming down through an opening in the trees, her face looked pale and drawn while the bruises on her face seemed darker.

"Hang on," he said, reaching out a hand and touching her shoulder. "It won't be much longer."

Lou turned to him, smiled faintly, and nodded. "I can make it," she said.

And she would, Tom Laverty knew. Lou Petty was made of strong stuff; she came from people who withstood all the hardship that a poverty-stricken way of life could visit upon them. He couldn't blame her for running away from it, for seeking something better. It was just unfortunate that, being young, she had fallen into the hands of a man like John King.

"There's the cabin," Zack called back.

Laverty strained to see the structure, finally located

it off to his right and almost hidden by unrestrained underbrush.

"Can hide the horses around back," the old marshal said. "Ain't likely to be spotted there if some of that bunch happens to come along."

Zack rode in close to the cabin, a solid-looking structure of weathered logs, and circling it, came to a halt. He left the saddle at once, and still in the fore, led the gray he was riding into the deep brush nearby. Tom, dissatisfied with the location of the place, feeling it was too near the town, put his misgivings aside, helped Lou off the sorrel, and followed Zack with their horses.

Hurriedly they dropped back to the cabin, forced the door open, and entered. The large, single room was musty from being shut up for so many months, possibly years, and each step they took raised puffs of powder-fine dust off the floor.

"We can see out the front," Zack said, pointing to a small window. "Door's nailed shut, and there ain't no other windows in the back or the sides."

Laverty nodded. "Like a fort," he said, and pulling up a bench, dumped it over to dislodge the dust on its surface and then, turning it upright, motioned for Lou to sit down and rest. There was no need for a light even if they dared risk one, for the brightly shining moon pouring through the one window and the open back door made it unnecessary.

"Not too sure I like being cooped up like this," Laverty said, watching a pack rat scurry out into the night. "They could pin us down real easy," he added as he crossed to the dust-filmed window and looked out.

"First got to find us," Zack said, "and there ain't much chance of that 'cause most everybody's forgot about this place being here . . . How's it happen you didn't kill Charlie Morral, too?"

Tom shrugged, wishing the older man would forget about the Morrals. "Was a fight. Shot him to keep him from using his knife on me. He'll be out of commission for a spell."

Fish sighed. "Too bad you didn't put him in the boneyard along with them other two Morrals. A bad lot, all of them." He turned to Lou. "John King do all that to you for running off?"

She nodded. "Would have done more if Tom hadn't showed up and stopped him."

Zack wagged his head slowly. "So you had it out with him too! You've been right busy for a stranger around here. Where's King now?"

"We left him tied up in Lou's shack."

Again the old lawman shook his head. "Like I said, for somebody just passing through, you've sure kicked up a lot of dust."

"And all just because he wanted to do a favor for my pa," Lou said. "Tom, I don't know how I can ever repay you for all you've done for me."

Laverty's wide shoulders stirred indifferently. "No thanks needed," he said, leaning closer to the window. A time later he drew up suddenly. "Something moving out there."

Fish stepped quickly to his side. "Probably an old buck mule deer. Lots of them around."

Laverty said nothing but continued to study the pocket in the brush beyond the small clearing that fronted the cabin. Abruptly he drew back. His eyes had caught the glint of moonlight on metal. Zack Fish saw it also: soldiers and armed men.

"Damn it," the older man muttered, "they're out there for certain. Must've been Rufus or somebody like him that remembered this place and hunched we'd be here."

Tom had turned. He didn't think the soldiers and the volunteers from Pardo had surrounded the cabin as yet.

"Zack, I'm taking your horse; mine's too beat to run," he said in a quick, taut voice to Fish. "I aim to try and draw them off, make it look like all of us are on the run."

"You go right ahead, take my horse."

Lou had come to her feet. Her features were strained and worry filled her eyes. "Are you sure you can get by them?"

"Got as good a chance of doing that as we have of staying alive in here," Laverty said. "I'll meet you tomorrow morning on the trail a mile north of Watrous. Keep in the trees out of sight. I'll find you."

"We'll be there," Fish said. "Best you be mighty careful."

"Aim to," Tom said, moving to the door. Hesitating, he glanced back at Lou.

"Good luck, lady."

"Good luck to you, Tom," she said, her eyes bright. "I'll see you tomorrow."

"Take a bet on it," Laverty said, and ducking low, passed through the partly open doorway and hurriedly crossed to the horses.

Singling out the lawman's gray, he swung quickly up into the saddle, listening into the night as he did. He could hear movement somewhere in front of the cabin, but with the exception of insects clicking in the brush, all seemed quiet where he was. The posse hadn't as yet gotten organized enough to take matters fully in hand, Laverty guessed.

Moving away from the other horses, Tom rode a few yards to the south. Halting, he drew his gun, and then raking the gray with his spurs, sent the horse plunging ahead into the trees.

"There they go!" he shouted, and fired off a shot. "They're heading south!"

The response was instantaneous. A strident voice broke into the gunshot's echo. "Right! Swing right! Follow them!"

Laverty rode hard and fast through the woods for a long hundred yards and then slowed the gray. He could hear the soldiers and the posse off to his left as they crashed through the brush in pursuit. A gunshot again broke the stillness of the night. Somewhere close by a man swore feelingly.

Tom, spurring the gray again, put him to as fast a run as was possible. He didn't know what lay ahead or what he might be getting into, knew only that he had succeeded in drawing the posse and the soldiers away from the cabin where Lou and Zack were hiding.

And it would be necessary to keep moving for a few more miles, get as far from the old cabin as possible. Eventually someone would spot him, see that he was alone, and realizing the party had been tricked, double back to the cabin. He hoped Zack and Lou would have ridden out by then and sought safety elsewhere.

"This way!" he shouted as the gray raced across a small clearing into a brushy swale. The gray shied wildly as a bird, startled by the horse's sudden arrival, fluttered sleepily off into the night. Tom calmed the gelding, rushed on. Raising his gun, he fired again. "They're still going south!"

Laverty assumed the ruse was working. He doubted anyone recognized his voice, since he had been around the settlement but a short time and had talked to only a few persons. It had fooled the posse and soldiers at the start, that was sure, but just how much longer he could hold their attention was anybody's guess.

The brush ended abruptly. Laverty found himself in the open. Over to his left a short distance, two riders broke into view. Laverty hauled up short.

"There's one of them—the marshal!" the man nearest yelled. "I recognize his horse!" Drawing his weapon, he spurred toward Tom with the other rider following closely.

Laverty cut about short and endeavored to double

back into the brush. The oncoming rider triggered his gun. Tom felt the searing pain of a bullet as it creased his forearm. The second rider opened up. His bullets missed by inches and made a clipping sound as they sped through the leaves of the scrub growth.

The first man fired again, the leaden slug striking the horn of Tom's saddle and ricocheting shrilly off into the shadows. Laverty, trapped, still yards from the dense brush, cut sharply about and faced the oncoming riders. Raising his gun, he snapped a shot at the man in the lead. The rider yelled, clutched at his shoulder and veered away. Cool, Tom shifted his gaze to the second man. He was coming on fast, triggering his weapon as he hunched low over his horse. Taking deliberate aim, Laverty pressed off a shot. The rider jolted, rocked to one side, and fell to the ground.

"Keep going!" Laverty yelled. He could see no one, but the gunshots could draw some of the others. "They're getting away!"

Reloading his weapon, Tom listened to the drumming of hooves and the crashing of brush as the rest of the posse and soldiers raced on by. Then, moving slowly, he rode to the side of the man who had fallen from his horse. The wounded rider was nowhere to be seen and likely was on his way back to Pardo.

Grim, a feeling of regret running through him, Tom looked down at the motionless, dusty shape. Killing a man was a terrible thing, a haunting thing, especially in this case, where the dead man was only doing what he thought was right.

Laverty frowned. There was something familiar about the coat the rider was wearing. Coming down off the gray, Tom rolled the limp body over. He drew back in surprise. It was John King. Evidently he had been able to attract someone's attention as he lay in the shack behind the Castle and get free of his bonds, then later join the posse designed to recapture Zack Fish, but he would care little about Fish; his hate and desire for revenge would be centered on Lou Petty and him, Tom realized.

Climbing back onto the gray, Laverty glanced about. He could neither see nor hear anyone, but that was no real assurance. There could be members of the party nearby who just might ride into the clearing.

And Tom Laverty wanted to engage in no more gunplay. Never in his life had he made such use of his expertise with a gun and killed a man—but since coming to this accursed hellhole called Sodom on the Mora, he had slain three.

No matter that it was in defense of his own life, that he had survived the incidents due to his ability, or that he had sought none of it. Three men were dead at his hand, and nothing would ever change that.

Swinging the gray about, Tom headed back into the brush, where he struck a course eastward. The sooner he got out of this part of New Mexico Territory, the better for him.

25

THE sun was just breaking over the horizon in the east when Tom Laverty rode out of the thick brush near the Santa Fe Trail that next morning. He had spent the balance of the previous night in deep cover, alert for signs of the posse and soldiers, but nothing had developed. Evidently the men from Pardo and the soldiers who had participated in the pursuit had confined their search to the country south and west of the town and ignored the plains country to the east.

Off to his right Laverty could see the settlement of Watrous. Hunger was gnawing at him and he would have given plenty to swing by the store and buy up a bit of grub to satisfy the craving, but he was unwilling to take the chance. He'd wait until he joined up with Lou and Zack Fish, then decide what to do about food.

He met the girl and Fish an hour or so later, a long mile up the trail where they had pulled back into the brush, well out of sight. They spotted him coming and hailed him.

"Sure glad to see you made it!" Zack said as Laverty dismounted. "We heard a lot of shooting, feared you'd got yourself into a pile of trouble."

Lou, eyes soft, greeted him with a smile on her lips. "I—I was worried."

Tom shrugged. "Trick fooled them."

"Then what was all the shooting about?" Zack

demanded.

"I fired a couple of times to keep them coming. Then later, two of them spotted me and rode up shooting. I winged one, downed the other . . . Sure obliged to you for the use of your horse."

"Ain't that blood on your arm? You must've got hit."

"Just creased me . . . There anything to eat?" Tom said, glancing to where a low fire still burned.

"Sure. We got coffee, and there's some bread and meat and such. We figured you'd be hungry."

Laverty frowned as he followed Lou and the one time marshal in behind the brush. "Where'd you get the grub?"

"Well, Lou here had a little in her grub sack, and then we stopped at Davidson's store in La Junta, picked up some more."

Laverty, squatting, poured himself a cup of dark brew from the lard tin in which it had been made. "You think that was smart? That posse or maybe some of the soldiers are sure to stop by Davidson's and ask if he's seen us."

"Let them," Fish said with a wave of his hand. "Told him I was taking the lady with me to Vegas. He hadn't heard anything about what had been goin' on over in Pardo . . . Any idea who that jasper was you shot?"

"John King," Tom said flatly.

A gasp of surprise escaped Lou Petty's throat, and then she sighed in relief. "Maybe it's wrong to say this, but I'm glad."

"So you plugged old King himself!" Fish said. "Well, to my way of thinking you done the country a big favor there, too. He was a mean one and crooked as a bucket of worms. The other 'n, the one you winged, know him?"

"No," Tom said, helping himself to the bread and meat keeping warm in a skillet. "Only thing I know, he wasn't a soldier."

"That's good . . . Where you heading from here?" Fish asked.

Lou Petty had moved in close to the fire and, using an empty tomato can, poured herself a measure of coffee. Squatting beside Laverty, she reached out and touched his arm as if to reassure herself of his presence.

Tom gave her a brief smile and nodded to Zack. "Like I said, I've got to go back to Cimarron, get my other horse. Guess I'll go on to Cheyenne from there—not going to be healthy in this country for me. What about you?"

"I'm thinking the same, so I'm lighting out for Texas. Got me a friend over there. Just wanted to say that if you'd changed your mind about Wyoming, you're sure welcome to come along with me—both of you."

"Up to the lady what she wants to do," Tom said. "Still aim to go on to Cheyenne."

"Ain't Gilmore and his bunch up there around Cimarron somewhere? Could run into them."

"They're probably back in Pardo by now, but I'll be

keeping a sharp eye out for them," Laverty said, rising. "Expect we'd better move out. Not smart to hang around here for long."

"Amen to that," Fish said, pouring what coffee was left in the lard tin onto the fire. Emptying the skillet also, he handed both utensils to Lou for storing away in her saddlebags. "Sure obliged to you, Tom, for getting me out of that picklement. Had about made up my mind that I'd soon be stretching rope."

Laverty took the older man's extended hand. "I owe you plenty, too, Zack."

"Maybe; anyway I reckon we're about even . . . Come on, girl, if you're going with me."

Lou, at that moment buckling her saddlebags, turned and looked at Tom questioningly.

"You go ahead, Zack," Laverty said. "She's riding with me."

EPILOGUE

LITTLE remains to remind one of Loma Parda, the small farming community renamed Sodom on the Mora by a frustrated army officer, that once dozed peacefully along the banks of New Mexico's Mora River.

Victim of a time when Indian trouble along the Santa Fe Trail was continuous and a civil war between the states was imminent, the building of a great fort nearby had become a necessity. Thus it could be said that Loma Parda was an unintentional victim of lonely men in a strange, hostile country where friendship and sympathetic company came at a high price.

Now only a few crumbling walls, empty, window-less buildings with sagging roofs, and weather-worn rock foundations that lie bleaching in the sun like old buffalo bones indicate where the village once stood.

Few things last forever, and the turbulent, unbridled days and nights that it once knew are gone except in memory. However, there are some who say that on warm, moonlit nights faint music can be heard coming from the forgotten, forlorn structures that housed saloons and dance halls, and the ghosts of men like Tom Laverty and Lieutenant Joseph, and numberless blue-clad soldiers, brims of their campaign hats fanned up, walk the dusty street beguiled by the smiles of such women as Lou Petty, while a quiet man wearing a star, shotgun cradled in the crook of an arm, stands in the nearby shadows keeping a close if futile watch over all.

Center Point Publishing
600 Brooks Road • PO Box 1
Thorndike ME 04986-0001 USA

(207) 568-3717

US & Canada:
1 800 929-9108